TELLING TALES

Totally Amazing Little Exciting Stories

From Northern England

Edited by Lynsey Hawkins

CW00607337

Disclaimer

Young Writers has maintained every effort
to publish stories that will not cause offence.

Any stories, events or activities relating to individuals
should be read as fictional pieces and not construed
as real-life character portrayal.

 Young**Writers**

First published in Great Britain in 2006 by:
Young Writers
Remus House
Coltsfoot Drive
Peterborough
PE2 9JX
Telephone: 01733 890066
Website: www.youngwriters.co.uk

SB ISBN 1 84602 591 5

Foreword

Young Writers was established in 1991 and has been passionately devoted to the promotion of reading and writing in children and young adults ever since. The quest continues today. *Young Writers* remains as committed to engendering the fostering of burgeoning poetic and literary talent as ever.

This year, *Young Writers* are happy to present a dynamic and entertaining new selection of the best creative writing from a talented and diverse cross-section of some of the most accomplished secondary school writers around. Entrants were presented with four inspirational and challenging themes.

'Myths And Legends' gave pupils the opportunity to adapt long-established tales from mythology (whether Greek, Roman, Arthurian or more conventional eg The Loch Ness monster) to their own style.

'A Day In The Life Of ...' offered pupils the chance to depict twenty-four hours in the lives of literally anyone they could imagine. A hugely imaginative wealth of entries were received encompassing days in the lives of everyone from the top media celebrities to historical figures like Henry VIII or a typical soldier from the First World War.

Finally 'Short Stories', in contrast, offered no limit other than the author's own imagination! 'Ghost Stories' challenged pupils to write an old-fashioned ghost story, relying on suspense, tension and terror rather than using violence and gore.

Telling T.A.L.E.S. From Northern England is ultimately a collection we feel sure you will love, featuring as it does the work of the best young authors writing today.

Contents

Bedlingtonshire Community High School, Bedlington
Clint Howey (14)   37

Berwick Middle School, Berwick-upon-Tweed
Jessica Borthwick (13)   38
Courtney Yule (13)   40
Charlotte Wealleans (12)   41
Callyn Inglis   42
Imogen Aitchison (13)   43
Ellie Waugh (12)   44
Lottie Perks (13)   45
Cordelia Scott (13)   46
James Davidson (13)   47
Megan Birkett (13)   48
Ross Allan (13)   49
Georgia Kerr (13)   50
Liam Wood (13)   51
Melissa Kenny (13)   52
James MacGregor (13)   53
Laura Doolan (12)   54
Michael Beveridge (12)   55
Lewis Andrew Cameron (13)   56
Alex Reavley (12)   57
Charlotte Hanson (13)   58
Dean Stephenson (13)   59
Sammy Pollock (13)   60
Sophie Harrison (12)   61
Keiron Logan (13)   62
Marcus Rudd (13)   63
Fergus Harkins (13)   64
Michael Binnie (13)   65
Samantha Neill (13)   66
Amber Windram (13)   67
Katie Joy (12)   68
Hayley Gilchrist (13)   69
Gillian Whittle (13)   70
Emily Haddock (13)   71
Steven Colquhoun (12)   72
Gregor Thomson (13)   73
Martin Hush (13)   74
Samantha Blyth (13)   75

Jane Gibbon (13)	110
Alex Thompson (13)	111
Nicholas Blaszczyszyn (14)	112
Julia Steele (13)	113
Sarah Haswell (14)	114
Jamie French (14)	115
Charlotte Marlow (13)	116
Nicholas Langford (13)	117
Craig Loughlin (14)	118
Danielle Purvis (14)	119
Stephen Page (14)	120
Tom Parker (14)	121
Chris Tyrrell (13)	122
Emma Robson (13)	123
Madeleine Hutton (13)	124
Danielle O'Connor (13)	126
Ben Littledyke (14)	127
Ben Nightingale (14)	128
Zoe Neasham (14)	129
Andrew Shuttleworth (14)	130
Chris Watson (14)	131
Carley Jackson (14)	132
Hannah Wilson (14)	133
Rachel Cook (14)	134
Ben Russell (14)	135
John Luke Jane (14)	136
Simeon Mitchell (14)	137

St Aidan's County High School, Carlisle

Bethany Hill (12)	138
David Armstrong (12)	140
Danielle Cannar (11)	141
Amy Graham (12)	142
Ryan Johnston (12)	143
Katie Murray (12)	144
Ken Wiggins (12)	145
Jamie Sanders-Fox (13)	146
Oliver Watson (12)	148
Chloe Ostridge (13)	149
Catherine Louise Bolton (12)	150
Michael Ballantyne (13)	151

The Creative Writing

The Mystery Murder

Jack Taylor carefully carried the cup of tea into the living room where his younger brother was sitting cross-legged listening to the old man's latest story. Ted Williams was sometimes better than television for entertainment. He could make the ordinary stories into the extraordinary and the boring into the most exciting, not only that but every story he told was different.

'Here boys, go and get yourselves a bag of sweets, ready for the next story, while I nip to the toilet,' he said, and handed them fifty pence each. Ted got up off the sofa and headed to the toilet after he'd told the boys to watch the road on their way to the shop.

The shop was busy but the boys managed to get what they wanted and made their way home for the next story. Jack was the first to enter the house as Jude followed. 'Ted, we're back,' Jack announced but everywhere was silent.

'Hello, anyone there?' Jude whispered. There was still no answer. *Where could he be?* the two boys thought. *We've only been away for five minutes.*

'Well that's strange,' Jude whispered.

The boys walked through the living room to the stairs then they stopped. Out of one eye Jack spotted the old man's body lying on the stairs. Jack phoned the police in a hurry, while Jude sat with Ted.

It wasn't long before the police got there. Jack gave all the information but it wasn't long before Ted Williams sadly died. The police thought he had lost his balance and fallen, but the two boys were convinced he was pushed, that it was a murder …

Jake Dawson (12)
Amble Middle School, Morpeth

Haunted Castle

Stacey's mum was taking Stacey and Latasha to a castle in Alnwick. They'd been looking forward to it all morning, then they were on their way. When they got there, Lesley (Stacey's mum), saw her friend and immediately started talking. Stacey and Latasha wandered off.

Stacey and Latasha loved it at the castle. They saw a small arched door and went in. As soon as they'd gone in the door slammed shut, they could hear it locking. They tried to get out but they couldn't. They shouted for help but no one came. The room was haunted, there was someone in there moving things around.

Then Lesley opened the door. Quickly Stacey shouted, 'Mum don't let the door shut, it locks and there is something creepy in here, moving things around!'

Her mum heard what Stacey said just in time and held the door open. They quickly ran out. 'Mum, don't go in there,' said Stacey.

'Where did you get to? I was worried. Come on, this place is creepy,' Lesley said.

'I know, but I want to go in the gift shop,' whined Stacey.

'Me too,' laughed Latasha.

So they all went in the gift shop.

The next day when Stacey and Latasha went into school they told all their friends about what had happened at the castle.

Latasha Hume (11)
Amble Middle School, Morpeth

The Horrid Woman

It was 7.20 on a Monday morning and Mark's alarm hadn't gone off. There was a knock at the door. Mark's uncle, John, went down and answered it. By this time Mark was awake because of the dog's barking.

His uncle came up to say that it was his mum. Mark said that he didn't want to speak to her, but he had to tell her himself, so he went down and asked her what she was doing here at this time in the morning, and that his alarm hadn't gone off yet. She asked to come in, so Mark let her into the home. A few minutes later she tried to drag him out of the house, but Mark did not let her. The police were called by Mark's aunty, Susan, and they were there in minutes.

The police asked Mark to go upstairs out of the way while they sorted things out. A little while after, the police came to talk to Mark and he told them everything that had happened. The police kicked his mother out and she drove away. Mark was advised not to go to school that day.

The police went back to the station and Mark stayed at home for the day. Mark was very happy living with his aunty and uncle up in Amble, but wondered how long it would last.

Mark Grey (11)
Amble Middle School, Morpeth

Lost

There was a boy called Joe and another called Matty. They were going on holiday at the same time on the same plane. They slowly became best friends. When they were getting off the plane they realised that they were staying at the same hotel.

When they got to the hotel, they collected their keys and found out that they were two rooms away from each other. As the holiday went on, they got to know each other a lot better. They did everything together. Then they decided to go on a volcano trip, so they got the bus up to where they were meant to meet their tour guide, but they realised that there was no one there. They saw a piece of paper on the floor. They picked it up and it said, 'Monday closed, Tuesday 11.30-9.30, Wednesday 12.30-9.00, Thursday closed, Friday 9.00-9.00, Saturday 10.30-9.00, Sunday closed'.

Then they realised that it was Sunday and it was closed! So they started to walk until they saw a cottage at the other side of the hill. They went and knocked on the door and the woman who answered said, 'I'll take you home,' and she did.

Mathew Gray (12)
Amble Middle School, Morpeth

Biting Back

The roof of the building looked unsafe and unstable. It was the roof of the building that Michael was climbing onto. The roof Nick had dared him to climb onto. The one he didn't want to go anywhere near and yet was almost on top of. Why? It was that thing they were learning about at school: conformity. But this time it wasn't about conforming to school rules. It was about conforming to Nick's.

They'd been friends since the beginning. The first day of school, when he'd come and asked Michael to play. He was playing now. Playing with Michael's head. Taunting and tormenting until he didn't know where his thoughts stopped and Nick's began. He stepped onto the roof. It creaked and groaned under his weight. The wood was damp and decayed. 'There, I did it,' he announced, looking down at Nick.

'Right, into the middle, you didn't go all that way to chicken out, did you Mike?'

He didn't answer, just took tentative steps towards the centre of the roof. He reached it and heaved a sigh of relief. He'd done it. Quickly he shimmied down the drainpipe and to the ground, where Nick was waiting. He retrieved his school bag and they walked home, trying not to show how sick he was feeling.

He lay in bed that night, thinking. All the times he had jumped at his friend's commands like an obedient puppy. Well not anymore. He was sick of being Nick's lap dog. He was biting back.

Anna Middlemas (13)
Amble Middle School, Morpeth

A Walk Home

It was a dark and misty night as Holly walked through the dingy forest. She felt scared and lonely. She tried to make herself feel better by talking to herself but as she looked back at the trees that seemed to be arching in towards her, she felt scared and sad. She walked on and thought to herself, she wished she had never gone to Megan's house so she would not have had to walk back on her own.

She carried on into the forest until she reached the end. She came to a big field with many cows and sheep in it. She'd always been scared of cows ever since she was little, as a cow had chased her through a big field just like this one.

She stood still for ages wondering if she could avoid all those cows, but there was no way past them unless she went across the field. She eventually plucked up the courage and walked through the field slowly, just in case another cow decided to chase her.

She reached the end, feeling a little more relieved and proud that she had overcome her fear. She then worked out that she only had a hill and another field to walk over before she reached her house. Feeling more confident, she walked through the grass until she got to the hill. She walked up the hill, then halfway across the field she stopped to catch her breath. In the distance her house stood. She could see that most of the lights were turned on. She felt happier as she ran the last ten metres back to her house.

As she opened the front door, she heard her mum and dad talking. She called into the kitchen, 'I'm home.' Her mum came walking through the passageway with a mug of hot chocolate.

After her hot chocolate she went to bed feeling as if she could tackle anything, and she couldn't wait to do it again.

Emma Wilkie (12)
Amble Middle School, Morpeth

The House On Grimlit Hill

What am I doing here? Why did I come? Was it excitement? A dare? Or just a spur of the moment thing? However it happened, I'm here now. All that is going to change - I hope.

Earlier that day at school, I was talking to one of my friends. We were telling each other some tales that we had heard about the *Haunted House on Grimlit Hill,* which is known locally as the *Haunted House of Doom.*

My friend suddenly said, 'Why don't we go there? Me, you and a couple of other people?'

'Er,' I paused for a moment, thinking about it. 'OK,' I said, quickly realising that I should have said no. Before I had a chance to correct myself, my friend had walked away.

You may be wondering why no names are mentioned. That's because if you know our names, the curse of the *Haunted House of Doom* will strike you.

Back to my story. The rest of the day went past quickly. In my mind, I was debating: should I stay safe in my home or go to a haunted house? I chose the haunted house.

On entering the house later that day, the door suddenly slammed shut behind us. Footsteps could be heard on the floor above. The floorboards creaked; dust came down from the ceiling. We tried to get out, but the door was locked. The footsteps got closer. My friends had been turned to stone, I was next …

Robert Pearson (13)
Amble Middle School, Morpeth

Cabin Crew To Doors

Russell was shy, he knew it, his friends knew it and his family knew it.

Russell opened his eyes. For years, Russell had dreamed of becoming a flight attendant and now he had his chance. He had to go to Newcastle Central where he had booked the 7.12 train to London. Then he was to travel to Luton where he was to go to the Britannia training school to do his interview to become a cabin crew member.

On the way to London all sorts of things were going through his mind, most of all how he wanted to do a PA announcement on the aircraft.

When Russell arrived at the centre, he walked in and saw his name on the notice board, along with the other people that were going into the interview room. He went in and sat down.

There were three other people sitting behind a long table. Alison, the crewing officer, broke the silence and spoke. 'OK,' she said, 'Russell, why do you want to be cabin crew?'

'Well, em, er, I suppose I don't really know,' Russell replied.

'Well in that case, go outside and we will call you back after we have made our decision.'

Waiting outside, Russell was nervous and he could only pray he had got the job!

The secretary told Russell to go in and with a fake frown, Alison spoke. 'We are sorry, but we can't offer you a job at Britannia.'

'But just hold on a minute! This is my dream, my passion, something I have always wanted to do! You can't just take it away from me.'

'Why didn't you say so? You are now crew. Well done!' Alison said.

On his first flight Russell walked down the cabin. He picked up the PA receiver and spoke, 'Cabin crew to doors.'

He'd done it!

Jeffrey Handyside (12)
Amble Middle School, Morpeth

West End Winners!

'OK Peter, from the top!' shouted Penny from the lighting box.

The cast and choir from the Alnwick Playhouse drama group were rehearsing for their latest show, 'Little Shop of Horrors!'

Pretty soon they were taking their bows on the final night. The Ronnettes were played by Jemma, Jasmine and Stacy. Audrey was played by Rebecca. The girls were best friends.

When the girls went to the bar to meet their parents, they were stopped by Mr Bigshot, who was a talent scout.

'Hey girls, would you like to be big stars?' Mr Bigshot asked the girls.

'Yes,' they chorused.

Mr Bigshot made them a deal they couldn't refuse.

The next year, the girls were performing 'Les Miserables' at the Theatre Royal in London. Rebecca played Cozette, Jasmine was Ebony, Stacy was Javert and Jemma was the main Lovely Lady. The show was a massive success and the girls were famous in a matter of weeks. The girls themselves were also a massive success and were touring all over the world.

They were going to all of the best parties and weddings and premieres! They even stayed in The Ritz! They were millionaires by the time they were eighteen, and they became legends of the stage and screen.

Rebecca Gray (11)
Amble Middle School, Morpeth

Super Shayne Show!

I was really looking forward to my birthday present from my mum. Tomorrow was my birthday and my mum told me that she had a surprise for me. I stayed up most of the night begging her to tell me what it was. She told me to go to bed. All I was expecting was swimming or bowling, but to my surprise, I actually got tickets to see *Shayne Ward!*

I jumped up and down in excitement and kept hugging my mum. She told me to get dressed so I dressed in clothes I had received that day. I did my hair up all nice.

When we eventually arrived, I sat and fidgeted in my front row seat. Then I heard applause. I turned and there was Shayne walking onto the stage. I screamed. Then he looked right at me and invited me on stage. I was gobsmacked.

He gave me a poster and his new CD and then he also gave me his autograph. Then as I was about to leave he called me back and the crowd sang happy birthday to me. I began to cry and Shayne put his arm around my shoulder.

He whispered happy birthday in my ear then asked me my favourite song. I told him 'I Couldn't Decide'; he nodded. I went to sit back down in my seat and he began to sing. It was the best day ever and a dream come true!

Jemma Henderson (12)
Amble Middle School, Morpeth

Phillip's Life

Philip was a boy who had a miserable life. He had busy parents and only a few friends. One morning Phillip got up as usual, got breakfast, as usual and brushed his teeth, as usual.

It was a normal day. When he went to school he got a zero in a test but that was normal. He went to his room and out of his window he saw a shooting star and made a wish to turn his life upside down.

The next morning he got up and had breakfast but it was not normal, it was cake with icing. He went to school but didn't brush his teeth. When he got to school all the children started to talk to him except his old friends, who seemed to hate him now. He took another test and got full marks

He was happy with his new life but when he started to get fat and his teeth started to rot, he thought about what had made his life like that in the first place, and then he remembered he had wished on a shooting star! Every night he looked until he could find another but it was no use, he had now experienced popularity, uncaring parents, no good or loyal friends and no warm meals, just cake.

One night he saw what he was looking for, it was the shooting star. He quickly wished to go back in time so he could tell himself not to make that wish, and there he was at the window! He quickly ran over and told himself everything and he didn't make the wish. He was happy with what he'd once thought was a miserable life, for the rest of his life.

Alex Forester (12)
Amble Middle School, Morpeth

School Trip

Stacey, Courtney and Cassy were all going to Ford Castle with the school. They were staying over for two days. Everyone was excited on the bus and couldn't wait to get there. Stacey, Courtney and Cassy were on coach A and their team leader was Mrs Smith, who had just come to the school after studying teaching. They eventually arrived at Ford Castle and were told to set up their things, then go to sleep.

Cassy was woken by a door closing in the middle of the night. She made her way to the door and peeked out. It was Stacey, creeping down the corridor with a little torch. 'Stacey! What are you doing?' whispered Cassy.

'Going to explore, come on!' replied Stacey.

Cassy caught up, but wasn't sure about exploring the castle on their own.

They went outside first and heard a faint banging sound. It kept repeating itself. Stacey started walking to the underground cellar. Cassy followed her. When they got inside, there was a loud whistling sound. Suddenly, Courtney jumped out from behind an old barrel. Stacey and Cassy screamed. 'Oh, you idiot. Why have you been scaring us all night?' shouted Stacey.

'What are you on about? All we did is stay in here waiting for you,' said Courtney.

'So who was that before then?' asked Cassy.

When they arrived back Mrs Smith was waiting for them, but didn't do anything and told them never to do it again.

So who was it that made the noises before Courtney?

Becky Lee (11)
Amble Middle School, Morpeth

Charlotte Gets A New Puppy

This diary belongs to Charlotte Mason who is fourteen years old and lives in Newcastle.

12th June, 11.30
Dear Diary,

I've just offered to wash the cars so I'll be better off, and by the way, if you're wondering why I'd offer to wash the cars, it's because I really, really want a puppy, so I have to save up. I'd better be off now, bye.

12th June, 12.30
Dear Diary,

I've finished washing the cars and it's taken me half an hour, that's ten pounds in the piggy bank, but I've still got a long way to go before I can afford a puppy. Tomorrow I'm going food shopping for my mum down the local supermarket and then I'm going to go to my gramma's because she's in a wheelchair. I'll tell you more about it tomorrow, because I'm going ice skating with my friend Beth. Bye.

13th June, 10.00
Dear Diary,

Ice skating was mint, especially when Beth's dad fell over. I'd better go because I'm going food shopping, remember, and then I'm going to my gramma's to help her. Bye.

13th June.
Dear Diary,

I'm back from my gramma's but I can't talk for long because it's 9.30 - I'm going to bed early so I'm not tired for when I go to my little cousin's house to sleep. Mum's going to hospital; it's time for my little brother or sister to come. Think I'd rather have a puppy!

14th June, 10.30
Dear Diary,

Mum's just come back from hospital. I've got a little sister named Lucy, but much better, I've got a *puppy!* I've named him Biscuit. Well I am off as we are having a congratulations party for my mum, and maybe we'll meet again sometime. Bye.

Kiera Baxter (12)
Amble Middle School, Morpeth

Spy Dogs

It was another successful night. Spy Dogs had saved Cuddles, the baby cat, from being blown up by a complicated time bomb. Cuddles' family could not thank them enough for saving her. They gave them chocolates, flowers and about a million dog biscuits.

The dog gang was Sparks, Charlie, Rascal and Tabs. Their home was in a warm barn with all kinds of devices. They had four useful computers, a satellite navigation system, you name it, they had it. Sparks was the leader of the gang.

'Everyone come over here,' gasped Sparks. 'We've got a reading on the computer that the nearby bank is being robbed.'

The dogs had never saved a bank before and were up for a risky job.

'Tabs?'

'Yes, Sarge?' Tabs replied.

'Check the security cameras on the navigation screen.'

'At your service, Sarge.'

The hidden cameras showed nothing.

'Well you never know, they might be hiding!'

'Let's get down there quick,' ordered Sparks.

The gang got down there and in no time they were in the back alley behind the bank.

'Now, everyone stay where you are and don't move an inch,' whispered Sparks.

'OK,' everyone replied.

'Hey look, a window,' Charlie shouted.

'No, don't!'

It was too late. Charlie had pushed the wooden window and forgotten about any booby traps. A small, bleeping noise echoed in the room beyond the brick wall and a small red light flashed at the end of the window. A few seconds later, a group of armed baddies approached them in a threatening manner. They did not have enough time to escape. The baddies were armed with explosives, bombs and weapons. Is it the end of Spy Dogs, or do they just think that?

James Fender (12)
Amble Middle School, Morpeth

The Great Bank Robbery

The date is 4th July 2003, location London.

Big Ben struck noon and a suspicious black van drove into town and parked outside the bank. Minutes later a man got out wearing a blue tracksuit and a balaclava. He walked into the bank and fired two shots in the air while shouting, 'Everybody on the floor.' He walked over to a bank booth and said, 'I want 100,000 now.'

A frightened cashier gave him the money while someone called the police. The man got away before they came.

The police arrived. An officer asked, 'What did he look like?'

The cashier replied, 'He had a mask on.'

'Well what was he wearing?' asked the officer.

'Erm, I think a blue tracksuit,' replied the cashier.

'We will try our best to track this man down,' the officer replied.

The next day the black van drove into town, it parked in an alley and five men got out armed with shotguns. The police approached the men but as soon as they got close the men opened fire and shot them.

The Armed Response Service were called and arrived soon after. Sergeant Josh, and his right-hand men Aaron and Jamie, were met by an alarm ringing at the jewellery shop so they immediately moved into position.

The armed robbers fled the shop but the qualified men were too quick for them and managed to catch them without a single shot being fired!

The men were sent to prison for life and the streets of London were a safer place to shop!

The three Special Armed Response men were all given medals for their bravery.

Josh Robison (11)
Amble Middle School, Morpeth

Head In The Clouds

Once upon a starry night in the kingdom of Dulock there was a man named Alex. Alex was your typical tall, dark and handsome guy who had a hobby of travelling and trying to be a hero. He had an apprentice named Alfred. He was small and had a hunch. He worked hard for his master.

When they awoke the sky was alight with fire and the screaming of people was deafening. When Alex looked to the sky there were dragons the size of waves. As he looked to the left there was a small group of men holding weapons and wearing highly polished armour. *It's the king's guard,* Alex thought to himself.

There was a clattering of hooves, it was King James VII in his black shining armour. 'Charge!' he shouted and a mass of men behind the hill suddenly sprinted firing their bows.

A shady man came out of nowhere, he was Josh the local dragon slayer, he shot down several dragons. I was just standing still. I could not move as a humungous dragon was coming, its fire was so destructive and in a second Josh turned to ash.

'Alex, Alex wake up.' It was Mrs Hover my teacher. 'Have you always got your head in the clouds?'

'Yes Miss!' I said.

Aaron Davies (12)
Amble Middle School, Morpeth

The Charge

'Hellfire Squad!' the sergeant shouted at the top of his lungs. 'We have got to go to the Magifere Space Pad,' he bellowed once more.

'Easy as a vegetable capsule!' Private Warmsley announced as the huge beckoning of the battalion filled the night air with the gigantic birds.

'And ...' the sergeant continued, 'the path is crawling with horrible creatures!'

'More like Ork Rock Caves,' Corporal Briggs coughed about to burst with laughter.

The day began with the burning sun, Maglir 2, entering the observation room with a sign saying. *Bless This Mess* inscribed on it.

As well as the huge trees of magifere that cluttered the skyline, the gigantic mountain of Hirolara stood firm.

After a brief wake up call the group of soldiers then walked twenty miles to the spaceport and on the way a mysterious thing happened.

It was a rainy day and they were about to cross the marshes.

'Okay lads we've got to get across this swamp without getting killed!' the sergeant instructed as the troops moved quietly along the floor until, *snap!* A sound heard far away but still a single soul heard it. As Private Warmsley turned his head a dark tentacle came out of the canopy of the trees and grabbed him by the neck and pulled him up, never to be seen again.

Eventually they did get to the space pad and flew off back to Earth ...

Adam Harvey (12)
Amble Middle School, Morpeth

The Monster Hunters

It was a cold night, much colder than any other night and Jim and Bob were called to check up on a reported attack.

When they got there they noticed a chunk out of the neighbour's car. They could smell a disgusting smell which they had smelt before.

They went inside. A woman and four children were lying dead on the kitchen floor. They got investigators in. One of them noticed a huge slash in the wall. 'This was no man, it was a monster.'

While they were going home they saw a huge, black, hairy beast going into an abandoned church nearby. 'We'll check it out tomorrow,' Bob explained.

'OK,' agreed Jim.

When they went back in the morning there was an appalling smell, it was utterly disgusting. They went in. The monster wasn't there.

After a while they got a call about another attack.

Again they were too late.

Then it clicked. The monster would be back at the church.

They went back to the church. They peeked through a tiny hole in the door. 'I have bugs crawling in my pants.'

Bob didn't pay any attention and lined up and shot at the beast. He was about to shoot when Jim bounced up and hit the gun. Bob missed the beast and it fled. Bob was furious.

The next day they came back and Bob shot the beast.

They were heroes of the town and they were named 'monster hunters'. Well Bob was, Jim just got in the way!

James Davison (12)
Amble Middle School, Morpeth

The Mysterious Girl

One dark and eerie night, I was walking along a quiet and empty road when suddenly I froze. There were strange noises coming from the alley behind me. There was a little girl sitting on a box crying. I went to talk to her and see if she would stop. She stopped crying and looked at me in astonishment. An elderly man walked out of the shop across the road. I turned around and looked at him, he stared at me in a weird way.

'Who are you talking to?' he shouted.

I replied, 'The little girl. Can't you see her?'

'You'll get put in the nut house if the coppers catch you!' he said.

'OK,' I said in a slow, freakish tone.

The man left and I looked at where the little girl had been sitting.

'She's gone!' I said, in amazement.

'But I was facing the only exit. She couldn't have left,' I said to myself, when something began to growl.

I was out on the road the next night on the way home from the club, when suddenly the car went out of control. The fuel gauge was going up and down, the car was spinning and the gear stick was moving all around. I looked forward. The car was spinning towards the edge of a cliff. I was screaming. The car went over the edge. I panicked. I looked up and all I saw was the girl watching me fall. I heard her laughing as I faded into the distance.

Emma Harrington (11)
Amble Middle School, Morpeth

The Lily Pads

In a small pond just outside a forest of tall green trees there lived a group of frogs. The frogs' most precious things were their lily pads which were always being stolen by the frogs' worst enemy, Charlie the mole.

In Charlie's hole they were debating if they should try and steal the lily pads once again. They started to argue that they had tried too many times. They finally decided that they would try again so all that night they were thinking of a plan to steal the lily pads.

The next night they set off to steal the lily pads not knowing that the frogs knew that they were coming. When they got there they took as many as they could then the frogs charged out. All the other moles ran off leaving Charlie, the frogs quickly grabbed Charlie and threw him in jail. The frog leader, Wart Face, was talking to him saying things like, 'Give us our lily pads back,' but Charlie refused to give them back until Wart Face said, 'We'll let you go free.'

Charlie said, 'Yes, I'll return them.' When Charlie got back to his hole he went mental that his fellow moles had left him on his own.

The frogs were very happy that they had their lily pads back in their pond where they belong,

'What would moles want with lily pads?' one of the frogs said to Wart Face.

'Who knows, moles are the weirdest creatures I have seen in my life!' Wart Face said, in a horrible voice.

Thomas Fellows (12)
Amble Middle School, Morpeth

Manic Man

Down Crockturtle Lane, everything was quiet until *bang!*

A bunch of thieves ran out of the main supply store and hopped into a car and drove away, leaving a fire in the main building. Unfortunately for the store owner, Mr I M Aturtle, he was stuck in the building with no water.

Fortunately, Manic Man was in the area, with his super water burst power, he could easily put out a fire, if he wasn't so stupid.

'OK, this fire can be put out with water, but how can I find water ...?'

'You, you idiot!' shouted the street crowd.

Manic Man listened, and remembered his powers, so he used them and put out the fire, but there was still the bunch of thieves to catch. When he listened to Mr Aturtle, he got the idea of who to catch, and he was off (as well as water elements, he could also fly really fast.)

When he found the car, he realised that his archenemy, 'The Dingo' was in for a showdown he would never forget. Dingo started off by using his incredibly large mouth to bite Manic Man, but M M countered by using his water arrows to hurt Dingo. It was a tremendous fight, but Manic Man triumphed by flying into Dingo at a high speed and knocking him out. Manic Man retrieved the stolen money and returned it to I M Aturtle. Manic Man saved the day.

Jamie Pringle (12)
Amble Middle School, Morpeth

Bob's Got Speed

One day Bob went outside with his pet mole, Moley. Today was the big day. The race was in an hour. Bob had to hurry up or he'd be late.

'Haway Moley!' said Bob. 'Get in the car.'

So Moley got in the car with Bob. Bob started the engine and they set off for the other side of Bobville.

Bob enjoyed driving his new shiny Ferrari Enzo, it was really fast and had a special seat for Moley. 'Just two miles left Mr Moley,' said Bob. 'It's only thirty minutes until the race begins.'

When they arrived at the rally track, Bob and Moley got out of the car and went to get prepared for the race. Bob looked at his watch. Ten minutes to go. He and Moley went to their garage and collected The Molinator (their car) and went to the starting area.

They were against thirty-nine other racers.

3 ... 2 ... 1 ... Go!

The race was on! Bob was far behind the other racers but he had a plan. He went around the outside and was in twenty-second place. Then he 'burned' another twenty racers and was in second. The crowd of stickmen cheered for Bob. He had to win. *But!* his engine failed. Moley tried to use his 'mole' powers but they didn't work.

Later on, they found out that a tortoise had won.

'Oh well,' said Bob, 'beaten by a tortoise.'

Robbie Carruthers (12)
Amble Middle School, Morpeth

The Seemingly Lost Ring Of Power

I woke up to a vigorous shaking: it was the butler telling me I had to get up. I could hear my father shouting in another room somewhere.

'What's ...' I paused, as I opened my eyes, the light stung, 'the matter?'

'Your father has lost his ancestral ring, it has been stolen by none other than Rosos the Desecrator.'

Even though the news stunned me I got up and went downstairs to the courtyard (we live in a castle you see.) My father, the king, was outraged and it must have taken at least an hour to get him reasonably calm.

'I know this is unheard of but I could go and retrieve your ring, if I take my sword I can kill anything in the forest of spiders,' I said.

There was a long silence.

'You may go,' said my father and with that the servants fetched my sword and provisions for the journey.

As I set off I waved goodbye to my parents. It took half an hour to reach the forest of spiders. Inside the cobwebs that clung to the trees perfectly matched how I felt: scared. I heard a rustling in the bushes. A giant spider skulked out. A state of rage overcame me but that didn't help much, the spider still managed to sink its poison fang into me ...

I woke with a start, it had all been a dream. I breathed a sigh of relief.

Alex Nolan (12)
Amble Middle School, Morpeth

The Girl In The Garden

When Rebecca moved into her new house or more like ancient mansion, she got more than she bargained for …

It was a beautiful summer's day and twelve-year-old Rebecca was in the garden. Suddenly a girl in old-fashioned clothes appeared out of a bush. She was pale, almost transparent, *very odd,* Rebecca thought. The girl didn't seem to notice Rebecca's surprise; she chatted away and introduced herself as Annie Jackson.

The two girls played happily together for a number of days until one day Annie seemed unusually quiet and miserable.

Rebecca couldn't sleep that night. She wondered what had upset Annie. Finally she drifted off, only to be woken by a crackling noise … *fire!* She ran to wake her parents. A fire had started in the attic! Within minutes the fire engine arrived and soon the fire was out. Nobody had been harmed but the contents of the attic had been pretty much destroyed. As they sorted through the objects, Rebecca came across a rusty metal box. Cautiously she lifted the lid …

To Rebecca's disappointment there was only a bundle of faded photographs all in black and white. She had a quick flick through them. Suddenly she came across a photo which turned her blood to ice: there was an unmistakable photo of Annie. She turned the picture over. In old-fashioned writing were the words: 'Annie Jackson died in house fire on August 9th 1806'. Rebecca screamed and dropped the photo. Today was August 9th.

Rebecca went outside to the garden every day looking for Annie but never again did she appear.

Hannah Duquemin (12)
Amble Middle School, Morpeth

The Furry Bundle Of Love

I have always wanted a dog. They are really cute and intelligent. My friend Jane has a Labrador; he is gorgeous!

'How was school Sarah?' asked Mum.

'Fine,' I replied.

'That's good honey,' Mum commented. 'Your birthday is coming up. What would you like? An MP3 player A Game Boy? What would you fancy?'

'A dog.'

'How many times! I am not getting you a dog. They need to be fed, taken on walks and looked after,' Mum said firmly.

'But I can do that!' I protested.

'Sarah!'

I have tried so hard and I have almost given up. What is strange is that I found a brand new book in Mum's wardrobe, it was titled: 'How to Care for Your Puppy'. How weird?

'Good morning, Sarah!' said Dad smiling.

'Happy birthday love!' Mum gave me a hug.

'Here is a present from us both,' said Dad. 'I know you will like it.'

'Wow! An MP3 player! Thanks!'

'There is a big surprise in the living room for you!' said Dad.

I walked into the living room. 'Wow! A little puppy! Thanks so much!' I screamed.

'Oh and here is a book on how to care for him.' Mum handed me the book that I had seen in her wardrobe. I looked down at the small, fluffy bundle of love. I smiled at him, and he looked up at me with his eyes full of love …

Laura Young (12)
Amble Middle School, Morpeth

My Simple Life!

I thought I was normal. I thought I had a simple life but that all changed when I was only five years old … my mum and dad split up!

I can remember them shouting at each other as I lay in bed upstairs. When I was around them, they tried to act happy but it didn't feel right. I knew there was something wrong. For ages they stayed together but I just knew it was because of me. I wished that they would be OK and normal again but it didn't happen.

One night I was woken by the shouts and screams from downstairs and then all of a sudden I heard the front door slam shut. I ran down the stairs, finding it hard not to trip on my long pyjamas. My feet scurried across the slippy floor into the sitting room where my mum was sat crying. She told me that my dad would be away for a while, but that while became forever.

I'm now twelve. My mum's happy with her new husband and baby and I'm doing fine at school. But I often wonder about my dad. Where is he; what does he look like; does he ever think about me? I ask myself all these questions but will they ever be answered? Will I ever know? Will I ever see my dad again?

All I have of him are memories - some good, some bad, but one day I hope to find the answers to my questions … I will find my dad!

Ellie Davison-Archer (12)
Amble Middle School, Morpeth

What It's Like To Be A Dog!

Have you ever known what it's like to be a dog? If the answer is no (which it probably will be) read on and find out how peculiar is it.

I'm Lucky the Springer. Firstly, we like having our tummies tickled, we love running and adore dinner time. We hate having our teeth cleaned, having a bath and being treated like puppies!

Humans. They are loving creatures but also slightly annoying. They do lots of stupid and humiliating things but they think they are being cute! They have lots of games but this is one of their favourites ...

'Stay.'

Here we go again.

'Sta-ay!'

This is ridiculous!

'Good boy. Now stay.'

So they can have a huge head start.

'Come on boy! Come on!'

We are away like rockets. We have to run to a certain point. They have a big advantage and are only about two metres away from the finishing line.

'It's a draw,' they pant when they get there but we dogs always have them by a nose.

Some humans can treat us like total puppies but when they are depressed or upset we are always the first to know. We know they are upset but they try to hide it. We can usually help ease the pain with a wagging tail here and a friendly lick there but some things we can't heal. We talk to humans but they don't listen. Humans never listen to us. It's not that they can't hear us it's that they don't listen.

I bet now you want to be a dog. If the answer is yes (which it probably will be) let us know and we will send you some stick-on ears and a tie on tail. See you at Crufts!

Ashleigh Jordan (12)
Amble Middle School, Morpeth

Nightmare Grave

Abbie's house overlooked Barnsley cemetery. As she looked out of her bedroom window, she could see the moonlit cemetery with its gravestones standing sinisterly. Abbie shut her curtains and got into bed. She woke up three hours later to a scream … then it went all quiet.

Abbie was a curious girl so she went to investigate. The night was cold as she stepped out into the street. When she arrived at the cemetery, a quick shadow moved and all of the lights went dim. Abbie was starting to get scared and headed back but when she got to the cemetery gate she heard another scream and ran up to the top of the cemetery to see what the scream was … then she froze.

Something was rising from a grave Abbie tried to run but she couldn't. Then she heard voices, 'Come, come.' It was as if she was being drawn to the grave. Abbie tried to run away but she couldn't she stuttered, 'What do you want?'

'I need my soul, find it or I will never go away …' said the ghost.

'Where is it?' asked Abbie.

'In my grave,' the ghost said.

Abbie had to dig until she found a blue jar and then she heard the ghost saying, 'Thank you.' She filled in the grave, and then headed back.

Then … she woke up, it was all a dream.

Amy Campbell (12)
Amble Middle School, Morpeth

The Haunted Hut!

Sarah and her family went on a trip to a castle. They were planning to have a picnic and spend the whole day there. Once they'd paid for their tickets they began to walk to the keep of the castle.

Sarah looked around amazed. She started to walk slower and slower trailing behind. Then she started to panic - she had lost sight of her parents! She went all hot, running, trying to find her family.

Later on Sarah was still looking. *Where are they?* she thought. Running around the castle, she came to the car park where she saw a woman walking into a hut at the bottom of the hill so she followed; looking to see if her family were in there. She pushed open the door and when she looked around - to her amazement the woman wasn't there! She ran out in a state of shock. When she came outside she met a car park attendant. Explaining her problem the car park attendant led her back up to the car park to wait for her mum and dad.

An hour later she noticed her family at the ticket desk where they were talking to the ticket sales man.

Sarah ran up to them and jumped on them and gave them a huge hug.

'Where have you been? We have looked everywhere for you!' Sarah's parents asked, looking relieved that they had found her though.

'You'll never guess what, I followed a woman into a hut at the bottom of the hill and when I looked in she wasn't there! The car park man helped me find you and he said that a woman had died a while back and haunts the castle. She is called the *white lady*, she used to live in the hut you see! Can we have the picnic now Mum?'

Domonique Scott (11)
Amble Middle School, Morpeth

Spooky Castle

Once upon a time in Manchester, it was Hallowe'en. Martin, Belinda and Monica were talking about where to go trick or treating and decided to go where no kid had been before, *Spooky Castle!*

It was 8pm. Martin led the way and Monica was at the back feeling mixed emotions: she felt excited, nervous, happy but scared at the same time. Belinda was excited to be one of the first kids to go inside, but nervous too. Martin was happy and excited, he didn't believe in ghosts or stuff like that, and wanted to prove everyone wrong.

Martin had a torch as it was foggy and you could hardly see anything. The atmosphere was gloomy and damp. They could only work out what the castle looked like when they were standing right in front of it.

The door opened itself with a loud creak, they tiptoed in and saw a big double door and there it was, a huge caterpillar, about 300 feet long. They ran up the stairs as it chased them, they hid in a room that was like a janitor's room but without all the cleaning equipment. Monica whimpered, 'I can feel somebody breathing down my back.'

'Oh sorry Mon I have always been a loud breather,' whispered Martin.

They came out and went in the largest room upstairs, Martin opened the door and a load of spiders came out. In the middle of the room there was a tarantula, bigger than you will ever see. Since Monica and Belinda were at the back they managed to run out of the house but Martin didn't survive.

Since that day no one has ever gone inside Spooky Castle again.

Nicole Stewart (12)
Amble Middle School, Morpeth

The Mirror Girl

It was a stormy, dark night and Chloe was sitting reading. Mum told Chloe that she was going to the shop. Chloe agreed to stay at home alone. Ten minutes had passed, then twenty but Mum still wasn't home. Where was she? 40 minutes went by, Chloe started to worry. *Flash!* went the lightning. Off went the lights. Chloe crept downstairs as the thunder crashed outside.

The door opened with a groan. As the lightning flashed, a silhouette appeared, approaching the door. The thunder crashed loudly. Chloe ran upstairs and dived under her covers on her bed. She was shaking with fear. Her palms were sweaty, but Chloe was curious, she had to see what was happening. She peeped over the duvet and nothing was there ... the door kept banging, open and shut. Chloe headed to her door and from the corner of her eye, she saw something in the mirror ... there was a girl sitting on the end of her bed. The girl had her back to Chloe. As Chloe approached the mirror, the girl turned her head, slowly. She had her eyes closed. The girl approached Chloe, who was petrified. The girl opened her eyes. They were white. *Click* went the door.

'Mum?' Chloe shouted. The girl disappeared. It turned out that Chloe's mum had seen an old friend and stopped to talk. However that didn't explain the girl. The image of the girl remained with Chloe for the rest of her life, but she never found out anymore about the mirror girl. Chloe never forgot that night and never will ...

Jasmine Grenfell (12)
Amble Middle School, Morpeth

Three Cheers For Sweet Revenge

It was past midnight when 'the man' returned home. The cars were still parked outside his mansion. The wedding should have finished hours ago. The man had let his brother use his mansion for his wedding. He hadn't even got an invite.

The man walked into the mansion. Everything was silent. He walked into the dining room. It was full of bodies. He went out to the pool. There were bodies floating in it. What had happened?

The man went back inside. Sat at the table half falling off their chairs were the man's brother Adam with his bride Jodie. He walked to the phone and called the police.

They promptly arrived and set up an investigation. The forensic team ran tests on the bodies and found there was cyanide in the champagne and all the guests had been poisoned.

One morning, a few weeks later, the police arrived at the mansion.

'Matt Turner,' they shouted, 'open up, it's the police.'

The man walked to the door.

'We are arresting you for the murder of 150 people,' said the officer.

It turned out the man was a schizophrenic. It was he who had killed all the guests. He had been engaged to Jodie but she had run off with Adam on their wedding day.

He'd wanted revenge!

He had allowed them to use his mansion for their wedding but had poisoned the champagne. The man's girlfriend Christina had gone to the mansion and seen the bodies. When the police investigation started she'd told them all this and helped to get the man arrested.

Megan Iniesta (12)
Amble Middle School, Morpeth

The Abandoned House

Amy and her friends were playing in the woods when they found a dark passageway. They followed it and came to a door, opened it and in front of them was a gloomy room; they stepped inside and turned on the lights.

There were cobwebs everywhere. They walked further inside to look around then suddenly heard footsteps coming towards them. They ran for the door but it slammed shut and then ... the lights went out!

They heard a scream and started to panic then ... more footsteps. They were about to hide when all the lights came on. They looked around and Jaz shouted, 'Abbie's gone!'

As they began their search for Abbie, the footsteps started again and the room turned cold. Suddenly a ghostly figure appeared and they were all terrified! They ran back down the corridor continuing their search. 'Where do you think she could be?' whispered Linzi.

'I don't know but I hope we find her soon,' said Kate. 'This place is creepy.'

They tiptoed down the corridor and heard mumbling behind a door. They opened it slowly and found Abbie tied up. 'What happened Abbie?' whispered Ashleigh.

'I was taken when the lights went out and have heard strange noises since.'

'So have we, and we've seen a ghost too!' said Amy.

'Come on, let's get out of here,' said Abbie.

They ran towards the door but a ghost started to chase them. They ran until they finally escaped leaving the ghost behind. They ran as fast as they could to Amy's and vowed never to go back again.

Amy Gair (12)
Amble Middle School, Morpeth

A Shocking Entry!

1st January 2006

Dear Diary,

Well today I'm starting a new diary and this morning was really weird! It all started today when I woke up and I found a note on my bedside table explaining that my dad had been called into work early as he's a nurse at the local hospital. My mam also works there, she's a surgeon, but it didn't say she'd been called in, but I just assumed she had since she had written the note! There had probably been a mad rush as it was New Year's Eve last night!

Anyway, back to my point, I got ready for school and made my way downstairs. There were no lights on and it was still pitch-black outside. When I was seven steps off the landing, the boiler clicked on, I must have jumped because I landed with a 'thump' and a sore bum at the bottom of the stairs!

Normally when I'm making my packed lunch for school, Mam and Dad are normally in the kitchen having breakfast, but this morning was the first time I had been left alone in the morning on my own! As I buttered my bread, a cool breeze ran through me, and then suddenly Mam's favourite mug fell off the side and smashed. As I swung round, my palms sweating, I saw a dark shadow moving slowly along the black corridor … into the kitchen! I started breathing really heavily, digging my nails into my wet hands, then suddenly … I heard, 'Pop the kettle on chick, I'm dying for a cup of coffee,' croaked Mam!

Rachel Common (12)
Amble Middle School, Morpeth

Darkness

It was Abbie's birthday and she was having some friends; Rachel, Kate, Ashleigh, Jasmine and Lindsay, over for a sleepover after taking them to the cinema to see 'An American Haunting'.

'That film was really good, spooky but good!' said Kate on the way home to Abbie's.

'Oh no! It's raining, we can't play out now!' said Rachel.

'Well it'll be pitch-black by the time we get home so I don't think you would be playing out anyway!' replied Abbie's mam, Leslie.

It didn't just start to rain, it started to thunder and lightning and it hadn't stopped by the time they got home.

Leslie went to Julie's to pick up Liam, Abbie's brother, while the girls watched the lightning flash. 'Wow, wow,' they chorused every time there was a flash. 'Wow, wow ... argh!' they screeched, the lights went out, the power was out.

Lindsay and Jasmine went to the window to find out the whole street was out. Everyone looked at each other's silhouettes trying to make out who was who.

The living room door creaked open ...

'Argh!' screamed Jasmine. 'I don't like this!'

They all climbed behind the sofa when strange noises came from outside.

The lock turned in the front door ... it creaked open and slammed shut ... footsteps walked towards the living room door ... the door opened ... lightning flashed! A little figure of a boy stood in the doorway.

'Aba!' said the little baby's voice.

'Aww, Liam,' said Abbie running over and giving him a hug.

'Did you girls survive then?' said Leslie, laughing.

'Barely,' said Rachel laughing.

Lindsay Smith (12)
Amble Middle School, Morpeth

The Scottish Wolf

On the road to Father Cuthbert's Chapel, King Charles was riding his faithful steed alongside his best friends Sir William and his guard Sir Edward.

'I do say, this road is awfully crooked,' Sir William moaned. He liked to moan. His hobbies included moaning, hunting, moaning, shooting - and moaning. King Charles ignored his friend. It was almost nightfall and they needed to get to the chapel before the morning sun came up.

'Come on, I want to go and see that Loch Ness monster!' King Charles shouted.

In the morning King Charles loaded his gun and set off for Loch Ness. Once he was there he pulled up a boat and started to row. Suddenly, he saw a dog-like creature on dry land. At first he thought it was just a dog, but then he saw it stand on its hind legs. It looked as if it were staring right at him. He picked up his gun and shot the creature in the chest. It let out a howl and ran off, limping into the distance.

That night the king encountered the beast again.

'That is it,' he said to himself. He picked up his gun, but before he could load it the beast shattered through the window as Sir William and Sir Edward burst through the door. Sir William shot him with a silver gun. Just as the bullet was about to hit the monster, Father Cuthbert shouted, 'Fall to the depths of Hell and never return!'

'Well, let's all get some sleep and we can go down to the loch and look for that monster,' King Edward suggested.

But whether they found it or not is another tale.

Sam Hunter
Amble Middle School, Morpeth

The Mercenary

'The mercenary surveyed his surroundings and his opponent Ganesh looked down upon him. He thrust his spear upward at the god.' The old man telling the story sighed, he was old, 82 years and 4 days old to be exact.

'Carry on, carry on!' cried the young children.

The old man carried on. 'Ganesh showed lightning fast reflexes and split the spear in half with a judo chop. The mercenary whipped out his bow and fired a full quiver at Ganesh, but the mighty God shrugged off the pain.

Ganesh lunged forward and tore the heart from the mercenary and sliced it into twenty pieces.

'Hinishi,' Ganesh boomed, 'your heart will be spread around India and only when all twenty parts are found can you return to the world you know and adore.'

The man finished the story and gazed at the younglings. 'They say that every bounty hunter in India gets this punishment, because they are willing to kill for money.'

'How do you know this?' a child asked.

The old man did not answer, he was fast asleep.

The moral of the story is do not kill to fill your pockets with money.

Clint Howey (14)
Bedlingtonshire Community High School, Bedlington

Material World

The excitement had been building up for months and the special day had finally arrived. It had been a tradition for several years, for the whole of Year 8 to travel down to the Lake District to spend four fun-filled days together. Maya and Piper had been planning their suitcases for months and had finally managed to pull the zipper shut round their bulging luggage.

Maya's mum drove the girls to school early, so they could see their friends before they left. As they pulled up to the school gates, they could see Emmie, the blonde-haired, blue-eyed most popular girl in school, in her brand new, white skinny jeans. Emmie was a show-off and she disliked Maya and Piper therefore, being a ringleader, she made their lives a misery.

As soon as the group arrived at their destination of Otter Scout Camp, they were given the names of those they would be sharing a room with. To their surprise, Maya and Piper were grouped with Emmie and her friend Carmen. 'I am not sharing a room with Emmie, she hates us!' exclaimed Piper, her red locks whipping her face in fury.

'You shall have to, Miss McKenzie, perhaps this might end your feud with Emmeline Roberts,' replied Mrs Terry, in a patronising tone.

The next few days were spent avoiding Emmie. Maya had just arrived back from an amazing day canoeing and Piper orienteering, therefore making their way to the pay phone to tell their families about their amazing day.

That night, Maya woke to the sound of sobbing. 'Psst, Piper, are you OK?' hissed Maya in a hushed tone.

'What? Oh I'm fine, yeah,' Piper leant towards her bedside table and quickly flipped the switch on the lamp.

The girls sat wide-mouthed, to their amazement they saw Emmie huddled at the edge of her bunk, crying into her knees.

'Emmie, what's wrong?' questioned Piper, as nicely as possible.

'Oh I'm fine, honest,' stuttered Emmie in-between gasps for air.

'Come on, Emmeline, you're clearly not OK. Are you homesick, do you miss your mum?' Maya pleaded.

'That's just it. I can't get hold of my parents, they're away in Japan. I never see them, they're always abroad. I spend 90% of my time with a nanny.'

After settling Emmie, the girls tried to settle down, but thoughts were flying through their minds. How had they not known? Emmie had so much but so little, no wonder she bragged about material things, she knew of no other luxuries.

Jessica Borthwick (13)
Berwick Middle School, Berwick-upon-Tweed

The Boy And The Bear

Anna rushed up to see the professor, splashing tea all over herself. It felt like microscopic leeches tunnelling deep into her skin, but she didn't care, her favourite thing in the world was visiting the professor. He was like a modern-day wizard. He worked in the museum there, but he was a born inventor, as he created all sorts of magical and exciting objects that did spectacular things. His room was cluttered with humming and twinkling objects that lay over the floor like ivy.

'Good afternoon,' beamed the professor as Anna flew through the door slashing a spherical object with tea, which fizzed and ejected thick yellow smoke.

'Mrs Short wanted to know if you would fix the leak in the toilet block, while the water's off?' remembered Anna, kicking the metallic object away.

'There, done!' exclaimed the professor after forty minutes' hard work. 'Do …' he stopped suddenly, staring at a small puddle on the floor under an old picture of a young boy with a bear.

'What's the matter Sir, are you afraid of water?' asked Anna puzzled.

'No, but am I correct that there has been no rain for weeks, and the water has been switched off in here for three hours now?'

'Yes,' replied Anna even more confused.

'Then what worries me, is why can I hear dripping and see water?'

Anna's heart hit the floor, he was right. That water wasn't there before. She glanced up at the picture of the boy, he was crying, real tears flowed down his cheeks. Real tears!

Courtney Yule (13)
Berwick Middle School, Berwick-upon-Tweed

Native Girl

Call me Tikal, and I live in ground that used to be mine because my father, Paramac, is the chief of our tribe. My mother died when I was young and the rest of my family is in the spirit world. The most important thing about me is that I can do magic. I noticed this magic when I was down by a lake and playing with an otter then the water started to dance and move to my hands, it did spirals, twists and turns. But no one used to know, as I was too shy to tell.

Then, one day the Caro tribe living close to us attacked us, a man named Manno tried to take the only thing that reminded me of my mother, a necklace, that is when I got angry, I felt my magic grow inside me, like a kettle ready to scream, then I imagined a huge wave taking the whole of the Caro tribe back to their ground and leaving us to live our daily lives. Then I felt it, the wave, I looked up, there stood the wave ready to attack, my father looked up, Manno looked up, nearly everyone looked up at the huge wave before them.

Soon the wave came crashing down on them, washing the whole of the Caro tribe away, I never knew where they'd gone but we never saw them again.

My father looked at me, 'Tikal, I want you to pack your sack and never return to this tribe again, I'm sorry but you are too dangerous for this tribe. Go.'

Charlotte Wealleans (12)
Berwick Middle School, Berwick-upon-Tweed

Room Number 12

The air was damp. I'm pretty sure we were going in circles, it seemed those were the only eyes to be seen in this spooky old mansion. Knights in shining armour and doors in disguise. It seemed alright when I first got there but then The Polka Inn got frightening. We were going there for the Easter holidays. It looked fine from the outside, on the website it had swimming pools, hot tubs and barbeques every other night of the week. When we got there the pool was green with mould and it rained every day. The only people there were the 3 people that worked there, a maid, a cook and the manager. Turns out those photos were taken in 1984 and hadn't been updated since.

When I got there I went up to the checkout desk and the lady said that my room was number 12. But there was a curse so why did she put us in that room if there were 30 rooms empty?

I decided to walk around while dinner was being cooked. While walking around I found myself at room number 12 again. I was pretty sure there wasn't a door next to it earlier that afternoon so I decided to take a look. Inside I found a box, it looked as if it was shining but there was no window nor light in the room so I left the door open only a little bit in case I wasn't supposed to be in there. I looked outside to make sure there was no one there. Then it slammed shut!

Callyn Inglis
Berwick Middle School, Berwick-upon-Tweed

The Big Race

The rain had poured all day, but now it was just a gentle drizzle. I gazed around at all the horses, I was definitely the smallest. My bay coat was hidden under my beautiful green rug with 'Red Rum' embroidered on the side. The speaker sounded for the horses to come into the ring. Just before my jockey was about to get on me, my rug was whipped off my back, as he mounted the last of the rain stopped. We walked over to the starting gate, the sun started to shine, I could feel the excitement rising up inside me. Horses all around me were prancing on the spot. Suddenly there was a loud ring, the gates flew open and we were off!

The crowd cheered as we galloped round the track. I kept in the middle of the group with other racing horses all around me. With only half a circuit of the track left I charged through the group of horses in front. I was in the lead and I could see the finish post up ahead, I was now only a few metres away from the post, the crowd were roaring, but I could feel another horse on my outside. *Snap*, the photo finish was taken and the race was over. But who had won?

My heart pounded as I waited, hoping it would be my name first on the winner's board. Just then there was a deafening cheer from the crowd. I looked up and saw, with my great pleasure, my name in first place.

Imogen Aitchison (13)
Berwick Middle School, Berwick-upon-Tweed

A Dog's Tale

When I was a puppy I was given as a gift to a little boy for Christmas. He didn't like me though. So that same night I was put in a small cardboard box and was left abandoned on a busy street in San Francisco. I was scared all night because of the roaring cars and drunken voices. That night I slept in the corner of the box so no one passing by could see me.

The next morning I was starving, I had had nothing to eat since yesterday afternoon. I could smell food all around. I started to whimper. Then suddenly a blinding light came into my box and a girl towered over me. That was the day I met Phoebe. We were the best of friends. Every day she would feed me, walk me and groom me. She was my owner and cared for me more than anyone had cared for me before.

The day I had feared so much had come. Phoebe had died. She was only thirteen but the cancer she always talked to me about had killed her. I feared what would happen to me and was right to. That night I was thrown out of the house and told never to return.

The first few days of living on the street were awful until I met Otto, a scruffy street dog. He taught me how to scavenge for food and how to fight. But Otto had disappeared and now I had to face the street by myself.

Ellie Waugh (12)
Berwick Middle School, Berwick-upon-Tweed

Do Dreams Really Come True?

One hot summer's day Leah was casually walking to school with her friends. Leah was very popular as she was the captain of the cheerleading squad. She loved to dance and her dream was to become a professional dancer. As soon as she walked through the gates she disappeared ...

Whilst her friends were chatting to the other part of the crew Jade noticed that Leah was missing. Jade told Ruby that Leah was missing, and they began searching for her. Jade and Ruby looked in the most obvious places such as the cloakroom and toilets, but after a while they found her staring at the noticeboard, which had different events and competitions happening.

'That's where you've been hiding?' asked Ruby.

'Oh, yes sorry I went off like that,' replied Leah.

Ruby and Jade stared at the noticeboard and discovered a dancing poster.

'Hey, look you could enter this!' shouted Jade.

Leah took the details and sent off for an audition. She could become a professional dancer and fulfil her dreams. Leah was really excited at school, and couldn't wait to get home. Wanting to get home really quick to tell her mum about this wonderful news, she ran home as soon as the bell rang. 'Mum, Mum, guess what?' screamed Leah as she ran through the door.

'What is it, what's wrong?' said Leah's mum, worried.

'There's a dance competition at the Stars in London, can I go please?' asked Leah excitedly.

Nervously, Leah steps into the audition room and begins to dance ...

Lottie Perks (13)
Berwick Middle School, Berwick-upon-Tweed

Spooky Sleepover

It was 7 o'clock and Natalie's sleepover was nearing, the excited party of 12-year-old girls, Anna, Natalie, Becca, Dione and Jodie, were getting ready. Anna panicked trying to cram everything into her small backpack, she gave a huge unenthusiastic sigh as she turned to face the massive pile of sweets and CDs which she was now regretting offering to bring.

Not surprisingly as it took so long for Anna to lug her stuff along the road, everyone had already arrived at Natalie's. Becca and Jodie answered the door looking terrified. 'Where have you been? We're watching some scary film, we nearly died when you knocked on the door!'

After terrifying themselves watching that scary film any unexpected noise terrified the girls. Natalie's cat, Sammy, scratched at the window, Becca and Anna erupted, screaming and clutching each other. 'You are such wusses!' Dione said with confidence, obviously realising it was Sammy at the window and then letting her in. 'There is nothing in this house going to scare you! Get over it!'

'Nothing scares you of course!' Anna and Becca mumbled sarcastically.

'You two infuriate me sometimes!'

'We know!'

Huffing and giving Becca and Anna nasty looks, Dione stormed off to the bathroom in a strop, locked the door then, out of the blue, screams!

'Must have looked in the mirror!' giggled Becca to Anna.

More haunted screams echoed through the house and Becca began to think there was something wrong. Just as she was about to go and get Natalie she burst through the door looking like she'd seen a ghost. 'We have to get out!'

'What?' said a confused Anna.

'Now!'

'What about Dione?'

'Move it!'

Grabbing Jodie the girls ran out of the house looking bewildered …

Cordelia Scott (13)
Berwick Middle School, Berwick-upon-Tweed

The Quest For Middle-Earth

There was once a great myth about a lair, Sheolb's lair, where huge spiders lurked and killed anything that entered. The mother spider, Sheolb, is the size of double-decker bus and as wide as a 20-foot swimming pool. It was the age of Middle-Earth where there was once great evil, which was led by the dark lord Sauron. Sauron had a fierce army of Orcs, Uruk-hai and a batch of evil men called Easterlings with a population of over 1 billion warriors. But Sauron had a special brand of warriors and his most loyal followers called Ringwraiths, their leader was a beast called the Witch King. Only one person had ever killed a Ringwraith and his name was Aragorn, King of Gondor.

On the second day of the 77th month of Middle-Earth in Minnas Tirith, in Gondor Aragorn and his most loyal companions, an elf called Legolas and a dwarf called Gimli set off on an epic journey through the wild lands to get to Mount Doom to create a symbol of peace of Middle-Earth. Aragorn was armed with the Nazghoul blade, a Gondorian bow and a hunting blade. Legolas was armed with 2 samurai swords and the elves' most powerful bow called the annihilator. Gimli was armed with a double-ended headed axe and a collection of miniature axes.

After the dark lord Sauron died the evil wizard Sauraman started to create a new army of evil-doers including the huge spiders coming from Sheolb. So on the way to create the ring of peace he decided to go into the lair and slay Sheolb. It was the 85th day of the 77th month of Middle-Earth. They'd entered the lair and and all seemed quiet, too quiet, when suddenly Sheolb jumped out on the three of them. Legolas drew his bow and started firing rapid shots at Sheolb, Aragorn drew his sword and struck Sheolb down. Then Gimli chopped her up until she couldn't grow back into the monster that she was.

James Davidson (13)
Berwick Middle School, Berwick-upon-Tweed

The Mysterious Night

'Bang, bang, bang. There goes that baddie!' exclaimed Lucinda as she was playing on her favourite game. 'Bang, get away from me!' She was doing really well and was about to beat her high score when, *Bang, boom!* The television exploded! 'Oh no!' screamed Lucinda, as she ran to turn on her bedroom light.

'Mum, I think the electricity's blown!'

There was no reply from downstairs, only a ghostly whistle. Lucinda ran to her bedroom door and shouted again, 'Mum, Dad are you there?' The only reply was her echo. She peered out of her window and the sky was a dark purple. She sprinted down the long, winding marble staircase. Her towering oak front doors were flapping open in the wind causing leaves to blow in her house.

She heard a smashing sound and whirled around. She saw her extremely expensive glass chandelier shattered to tiny pieces on the floor. 'Mum, Dad, where are you?' Lucinda called desperately. She noticed it was getting extremely late - past her bedtime. 'Mum, Dad, I'm going to bed now, goodnight.' Her voice was cut suddenly, cut out by a slamming sound. By this time she was too scared and worried to go to bed. 'I have to be brave, for my mum and dad,' she whispered to herself.

She started to climb back up the winding staircase when Lucinda heard something very strange. 'Lucinda,' a ghostly voice called.

'Who's there?' Lucinda replied.

'Turn around and you will find out!' Lucinda turned around and that is when she saw the monster who had captured her parents ...

Megan Birkett (13)
Berwick Middle School, Berwick-upon-Tweed

Is Something There?

In the dark night as the branches were swishing, they swayed from side to side as I walked through the old path, with my dog in the wood.

I heard a rumbling, scuffling sound behind me or was it coming from the side? I didn't know. I began to quicken my pace as my heart started to thump, the dog's ears and hair stood up on end. As I sprinted, I tripped over a branch. I wasn't sure who let out the loudest scream, if it was the dog or I.

The dog barked and barked. I think I had frightened him. I lay on the dusty ground for a few seconds very frightened. I jumped up as quickly as I could. I did not dare look behind me.

There was someone walking through the woods. What was surrounding me? Was it long grass or bushes, or something else? It was getting nearer and nearer. My heart began to thump, it seemed very loud.

I was so scared I couldn't shout or do anything. When suddenly, the old brown horse in the field, with his shaggy mane put his head through the broken fence, with his eye shining like a star in the sky. I was so relieved; I couldn't believe what I had been feeling after all the worrying.

I was just hearing and seeing things next to me. I am glad that my cuddly dog and me are safe, and that we both made it back in one piece.

Ross Allan (13)
Berwick Middle School, Berwick-upon-Tweed

Loner

My hand was nearly frozen stiff now. As I stretched my coal-black, dirty hands out in a plea for money. People find it so easy to turn the other cheek. I sat on my blanket, well rag if I'm being honest. I'm waiting for my mum, she should only be a minute now considering she's been gone six years now. Even though she's likely to be dead I still have hope, it's what keeps me from dying too.

I'm a young eleven year old boy and I already know how to survive, pretty responsible eh? My name is Semone and the only thing I wish for is a family. Families seem so wonderful, I see them walk past hand in hand sometimes wearing matching coats, cheesy but still cute.

I get quite scared at night, as people are mysterious but then again I'll look scary to them too.

This night was different though, I was asleep and someone pulled me off my blanket and hugged me repeating, 'You poor soul, you poor, poor soul.' I can't remember most of how I got there, but I'll cut it short she put all my things in a bag and walked me to a little cottage thirteen blocks away.

'In the morning I woke up with two little kids poking at my stick-thin body. Afterwards came the woman with the most delicious food on a tray. I was in Heaven. Since that evening I've lived here. Now at the age of thirteen, I receive an education, food and what I wanted most - a family.

Georgia Kerr (13)
Berwick Middle School, Berwick-upon-Tweed

Plan To Be Plotted

One evening in June a small skinny boy called Liam Cloudy woke suddenly. He woke up sweating, although he was cold, he had a shooting pain in his neck although nothing had happened to him, and he had the feeling he had woken from a dream but there was no dream. Liam wasn't normal, he was far from it, and you see Liam was what you call a ... Squib.

A hundred miles away a most evil plan was being plotted. A small, old, green, half-dead man called Wormtail Crookback was plotting a plan. The plan he was plotting was to kill Liam Cloudy!

Liam hadn't done anything to upset Wormtail Crookback into coming after him, it was his parents, you see Liam's parents were dead, they were killed by Wormtail Crookback, Liam's parents like any others were good people, they worked for a small company called Stingray Incorporated, with Crookback was the manager. And to complete his bidding he wants young Liam Cloudy killed.

Liam was now living with his grandma and grandpa. They were kind but they could be a right pain.

Liam was walking to school one day when Wormtail, disguised as an old man, asked for directions. When Liam had been kind enough to give him them he asked if there was anything else he needed. Wormtail replied, 'Yes there is one thing, and that thing is you Liam.' Wormtail suddenly grabbed Liam and in a flicker of an eyelid they were both gone ...

Liam Wood (13)
Berwick Middle School, Berwiok-upon-Tweed

A Day In The Life Of A Greyhound

It's 8 o'clock and my eyes flash open as one of the humans puts the radio on to wake us up. I wake up first but Storm (my kennel mate) takes ages. 'Tess,' from a loud voice above me, 'time to go into the paddock,' (an enclosed area of land that we play in).

I prance around the paddock with Storm, who eventually gets up, whilst the humans sweep and mop my kennel. Three hours later they put us back in and I have a quick snooze before lunchtime.

For lunch, well tea but at lunchtime, we have special greyhound food with all the nutrition we need in it. On special occasions eg Christmas, we get cheese or leftovers instead.

Sometimes I go racing. I don't really like it much because I never seem to catch the hare, no matter how fast I run.

My mum, Solo Flossy, was a great racer. I have two sisters and three brothers who live in the kennels with me.

My friends are Storm, Brandy (kennel opposite) and Jamela (kennel opposite). My hobbies are racing, barking, growling, eating, sniffing, chasing my tail and sleeping. My favourite food is cheese. My favourite types of music are dance and hip hop because it's something I like to wag my tail to.

After tea, everyone is full. I'm usually that full that I go straight to sleep. Sometimes I wake up when Storm's dreaming. He growls, kicks and rolls around a lot during the night. I just curl up and fall into a deep sleep.

Melissa Kenny (13)
Berwick Middle School, Berwick-upon-Tweed

A Plain White Dream

Bang, bang, boom! We all quivered inside our house as we heard all of the shells going off outside of our house. 'The blasted Germans are bombing again,' exclaimed Marie.

I felt the floor shake below me, we were all terrified. I hid under the bed covers. They were lovely, soft and smooth. Suddenly I saw a bright light appear under the bed covers! *What is happening?* I thought in my head.

I pulled the covers away to see nothing there but just a plain white room. Not a thing out of place. No dust, no cobwebs, nothing, everything was perfect. I got out of my plain white sheets and noticed that I was in white nightwear!

It was all very confusing because I hadn't changed and the room was totally different, what was happening? Was something playing with my mind? I started to walk around to get the feeling back in my legs. I thought of only one problem now, how could I get out? Would I starve? I started to search the walls for a way out but there was nothing, I was trapped!

Surprisingly the floor where I was standing just fell in and I landed in another room exactly the same as before! Were my eyes deceiving me or was I just crazy?

James MacGregor (13)
Berwick Middle School, Berwick-upon-Tweed

A Day In The Life Of Miles Longsette

Miles gets up after his mum comes up and threatens him with a bucket of cold water. After he finishes his facial art he retreats to his wardrobe and pulls out his black, baggy jeans and pulls them on.

As he puts them on he can feel his stomach rumbling. He is very hungry but he never has any time for breakfast.

With his good luck, he arrives five seconds before the bus comes round the corner. He jumps on, showing the bus driver his pass and says nothing as he sits in an empty seat thinking of the school day ahead of him.

When the bus gets to Suffield Square, Miles gets off, as it is a five-minute walk to the school. He strolls through the gate and stands one foot quenched up onto the wall behind him. He knows what is going to happen next.

He looks at the girls in pretty, flowery clothes; they are standing at the wall on the other side of the playground. The boys at the other side of the playground are in stylish pink designer shirts. It is going to be one long day for him.

When he gets into the classroom he makes friends with the girls and the boys that he isn't normally friends with and has a really good day.

He gets home and goes straight to bed because he gets in really late and dreams about his great day.

Laura Doolan (12)
Berwick Middle School, Berwick-upon-Tweed

Legless Larry

One day I was walking along the road when I just caught sight of the haunted house in the corner of my eye. It is the haunted mansion of legless Larry, but also I saw something hanging from the window, it looked like a person. I ran up to the house, there was a tall metal fence around it with a gate. I walked forwards through the gate with an annoying crunching below me of leaves that had been lying there for years. I walked up to the door, I touched the handle then it fell off, I pushed on the door and it opened slowly, I stepped in. I heard screaming from upstairs.

I went upstairs, the stairs were old and unstable. I was now at the top of the stairs. I saw the thing. I sprinted into the room and grabbed it. It was a voodoo doll of myself, I started to weep then something tapped me on the shoulder. I started to have a nervous breakdown. I saw legless Larry. I thought it was just rumours but he's real. He was coming towards me, I started to step back until I fell through a magic mirror. I fell in a heap at the bottom, I could hear him coming, there was a door on the left, I ran through the door. Suddenly I saw lots of people locked up in cells. I found some keys and tried to free them. *But then something grabbed me ...*

Michael Beveridge (12)
Berwick Middle School, Berwick-upon-Tweed

Colony 101

The siren cut through the air like a blade. She knew that she would have to hurry. It would begin soon and if she wasn't home or at least inside, she would die. She pulled up her collar and started to run. At least a minute had passed and she had maybe seconds left. She wasn't going to make it; she needed somewhere to hide, but where?

She had decided that she would never get home. So she had run in here, entertainment module 81. Inside she had found an old Chinese man.

'Wait a minute,' cried Emily. Something didn't fit. The siren had been going for twenty minutes and still it had not begun. She spun around and saw what she had been dreading. There were three people walking into the module. Their walk was mechanical; they knew what they were doing. And they were heading straight for the room that she was in, and for her. 'Hide me,' she cried.

'Why ever would I do that?' he sneered.

'What do you mean?' choked Emily, fear rising inside her. Just at that moment there was a knock on the door. Emily spun round and burst through, one of the people pulled an evil-looking gun from his jacket! She dived under the bar. One of the projectiles hit the wall and burst into flames, the other hit the bar itself and exploded. Emily flew through the air and banged her head. She looked groggily up and the last thing she saw was three figures looming over her, and then nothing.

Lewis Andrew Cameron (13)
Berwick Middle School, Berwick-upon-Tweed

Day In The Life Of An International Rugby Player

You wake up after a day of hard rugby and, even though you are exhausted, you are urging to play the game you have wanted to play professionally since you were young. The two kinds of rugby, which are very different from each other. One league and the other union.

The best game in the world is rugby and the game has everything in it. Pace, power, continuity and the flow of the ball are all the essentials in the game. People and fans ask me, 'Why do footballers get more money when rugby is a harder game to play?'

But I answer strongly, 'It's not about the money, it's about the love of the game.' Injuries ... well injuries are the most common thing in rugby and when they happen to you and your teammates it is very frustrating.

The training for the game is very important because it helps your physical and mental health, also it gets your brain and body psyched for the weekend or coming game. Whatever position you play there is a huge part to be played, for example a full back. If an attacker breaks the defensive line it is the full back's job to stop him. In other words he is the last line of defence. The game is hard, fun and easy at most times. But when the real thing happens it's time to play intensely.

After the game you rest your tired muscles in a scalding shower and that is the hard bit over for a while.

Alex Reavley (12)
Berwick Middle School, Berwick-upon-Tweed

Lisa

When Lisa was born her mother died giving birth and her father had already died three months before Lisa was born. Her father died at war. After four days in the hospital Lisa was put into care.

On Lisa's seventh birthday a Chinese family came to adopt her. She went with her new family back to China. After settling in her new home Ayer went to town to show Lisa around the town. Lisa found the town really nice.

When they got home Lisa had a look around the garden. In the garden there was a swimming pool, dog kennels and a stream that ran straight through the garden. As Lisa turned around she saw a path, but the path was covered with bramble bushes. As Lisa crawled through the bramble bushes she cut her face on some of the thorns. When the path came to an end there was a great big cave.

Lisa went into the cave. It was dark and cold. As she was about to leave a loud deep voice said, 'Watch out tomorrow big trouble is waiting for you.' But Lisa couldn't say anything. There was a bright light and the person was gone. Lisa ran into the house and told everyone what she had found out.

When Lisa told everyone nobody believed her that big trouble was waiting for her and about the man. She was sent to her bed.

The next day she woke up. It was normal. Everything was the same until a tall man walked in and said, 'I have something to tell you. You're a witch.'

'Nooo!'

Charlotte Hanson (13)
Berwick Middle School, Berwick-upon-Tweed

Siberian Terrain

The sea was rough and the waves hammered against the ship. Captain Micki Seel knew this was going to be a long journey, it would take at least eighteen hours and he wasn't looking forward to it.

Micki sat in his cabin when the door slammed open. In walked Sergeant Nick Roberts. In his left hand, was a dark blue folder containing the information he has been waiting for. It was the current whereabouts of the guerrilla's hideout.

Micki made Nick a cup of coffee, as Nick opened the folder, sprawling the maps and documents onto the large wooden table in the centre of the room. For the next three hours they studied and discussed the information which they had managed to obtain. Now it was time for the plan of action.

The next morning Micki told his soldiers what they were to do. They got into the helicopter, the brisk wind wailing against the side. The helicopter jittered as an icy blast hit the tail rotor but the pilot managed to keep it under control and stop it from plunging into the icy water below.

With half an hour left before landing, Nick, Micki and the other six soldiers in their group were ready for action. The weather was cold and the snow on the hard, frozen ground was six inches thick. The helicopter landed with a jolt as it hit the rocky ground. One by one they stepped out into the perishing weather.

Dean Stephenson (13)
Berwick Middle School, Berwick-upon-Tweed

A Day In The Life Of Tanna Wilson

On a school day I get woken up at 7.15 by my alarm clock. Then I go for a shower to wake me up a bit more! By the time I'm out of the shower it's 7.30 and my mum has ready for me a bowl of Kellogg's Clusters. After I have finished eating my cereal I get organised for the rest of the boring school day. At 8.00 I walk down to school, which takes half an hour because I talk to my friends.

When I arrive at school I meet some more of my friends there, Natasha, Holly, Meghan and Hannah. My favourite part of the school day is break and lunch but my favourite lessons are PE, English and LCT because they are the easiest subjects to do. My least favourite subjects are geography and science because I find it hard to remember all the information. I go to a high school and the bell rings to go home at 3.15.

My family is very large. I have a mum, stepdad, a sister, two brothers and an older stepbrother that is married. I see these people a lot because we are very close! I don't have very amazing pets but I do have a goldfish called Mary.

In the evenings I like to watch a bit of TV, my favourite programme is 'Doctor Who'. I also like to go on the computer and listen to random music. I also like to watch the TV in my bedroom.

Sammy Pollock (13)
Berwick Middle School, Berwick-upon-Tweed

The Lost Unicorn

Now I'm sure you've heard of unicorns before, but I bet you have never heard of one quite like Biblo before. You see Biblo was different in many ways, but there was one main difference, you could hold this unicorn in the palm of your hand. And do you know it's surprising you have never seen this unicorn before because he lives right under your feet. Have you never noticed how things seem to 'mysteriously' disappear?

Well, one day Biblo got into a bit of trouble. And I am on his trail so I'll let you see his diary as I found it.

I must be very, very quiet now. I am just about there. Argh! No, wait. What's this? Footsteps coming towards me. But I thought this house was abandoned. I have been here many a time before. No wait! Nooo!

I was trapped in a glass jar. It smelt of strawberry jam and was not quite clean. Luckily the mysterious kidnapper had put holes in the top. They mustn't have wanted me dead or they would have just killed me right there on the spot.

Suddenly, the doors flew open and two huge men with grizzly faces and scruffy hair reached into the van and grabbed the jar.

Outside it was bright and colourful and very, very noisy. There was a huge mouse in a cage and only a small bowl of water.

And that's where his story finished. He must have dropped his diary. I found it on the outskirts of the city. And now I will have to follow that freak show to wherever it goes. This is not going to be easy.

Sophie Harrison (12)
Berwick Middle School, Berwick-upon-Tweed

The A-Team

Steve smirked and looked at his companions. Then, turning to me he said, 'So you reckon you're good enough to be one of us then, Ben.'

I was trembling inside but looked him straight in the eye and said, 'Yeah, I've got what it takes to be one of you guys.'

These guys were the top in the school. Steve along with Emma, Chip and Sam were the 'A-Team'. They could run faster, looked better and had everything money could buy compared to anyone else. I was desperate to be one of them.

Of course, they could be arrogant and cruel, but I just accepted that was a part of being the elite. I wanted to feel superior just like they did. They were all filled with ambitions to be the best and I had to have the same.

The leader was Steve, he was the biggest and best athlete in our school. The boys all admired him, and the girls flocked around him. Although not as intelligent as Chip, or dare I say, myself, he had a natural air of authority about him. When he spoke you listened.

'Well, to join us you'll have to go through our little initiation ceremony,' said Steve. The others looked at him slightly puzzled. Steve had obviously thought of this by himself.

I replied, 'Sure, whatever it takes, I can handle it.'

Steve beckoned to the others to join him in a private conversation. I felt a bit awkward but kept up my look of confidence …

Keiron Logan (13)
Berwick Middle School, Berwick-upon-Tweed

The Dream Of Football

There I was playing for my club, Kenya Football Club. I had been waiting for this moment to play in a final. It was better than my favourite unbelievable cartoon. But there was a lot more than silverware to be won. There was also a contract to play for an English club next season for the player who was man of the match. We were playing the Mongo Lions. They were top of the league and we were second bottom of the league. We were playing our last game of the season and we're going down to Division One.

The manager talked to us and said, 'Play your best - all of you, because we're the underdogs and if we play a good game it would be classed as a good effort.'

As we walked onto the pitch the fans on both sides were calling my name. The ref blew his whistle and the match began with Mongo Lions. A good shot hit the post, went in and we were 1-0 down. After that I shot at goal but I hit the bar and Kenneth tapped in. It was 1-1. At half-time it was still 1-1. I think we were lucky because we should have been losing.

As we kicked off the second half, I had a shot and scored. It was 2-1 to us. But as the game went on we should have been 4-2 down but in the last minute I scored a stunner of a goal. We had won the game!

Marcus Rudd (13)
Berwick Middle School, Berwick-upon-Tweed

The Troll Heist

When someone says troll you'll probably think of a small, fat and dirty person but you couldn't be so wrong. Like everything they've evolved but evolution couldn't stop them being small.

Many are celebrities and other trolls earn their money in different ways like crime and these trolls don't just steal old ladies' bags.

We're following one of the trolls that stole £40m from a Securitas depot in Tonbridge.

It was no normal day for Dan Geris. He was going to commit the biggest robbery in British history. He woke up early because he was so excited about it. He already was rich from minor bank robberies and he loved his house. He walked across the kitchen to get his Weetabix and orange juice, cursing that he couldn't get a small fridge and cupboard.

At half ten he left his designer apartment in a pinstripe suit, heading for Great Portland Street station. He snuck into one of the dirty janitors' closets to meet his cronies, Eve Hill and Robyn Mayblind.

They discussed their million pound plan. Eve, because of her size, would find a way in and let the rest in. The others would drive the Subaru in, pick up the money and hide out somewhere. After the dust had settled they would go to the land of hope and glory, America. In Hollywood they would buy the house used by the Oompah-Loompas when filming. If this failed they would run away with the circus.

Will they pull it off?

Fergus Harkins (13)
Berwick Middle School, Berwick-upon-Tweed

Who's He?

We walked along the cliff edge at Lighthouse View. The wind was blowing a gale and every now and then we would get blown into each other. We came upon a rickety old house, which looked as if it had been there for centuries. David, Keeza and Alex ran up to the house. The door was swinging open and smashing against the rock on the outside of the frame. 'Come on then Alex,' said David.

'Fine then - as long as you come in too.'

They crept into the house, not knowing what to expect. They walked into what seemed to be the kitchen. Everything was covered in layers of dust and some of the ornaments were smashed on the floor from where the wind had blown them over. There was a huge Aga with mouldy food on it that smelled like a public toilet. Keeza decided to walk through to another room. It had a TV and a sofa, which had huge gashes in it where some sort of animal had been ripping it apart.

David looked out of the window and saw a shadow. He shouted, 'Come on you lot, let's get out of here.' They ran outside only to find that a scruffy old man, who had rips in his clothes, had blocked the door. They turned back and legged into the house and climbed out of a window at the back of the house. They thought they were away but the man caught them. 'You're coming with me!'

Michael Binnie (13)
Berwick Middle School, Berwick-upon-Tweed

The Alleyway

As I walked through dark, empty alleyway, I heard some strange noises that I could not recognise. It was getting louder and louder as I got closer and closer to the gloomy gate overgrown with weeds. The gate creaked as I opened it, I saw a shadow quickly escape, I panicked. I shouted for help. All of a sudden, someone ran behind me and pushed me in, locked the gate and ran before I could see who it was. I began to cry with fear. I was now panicking, I knew there was only me and this shadow in a dark, gloomy garden. The noises I was hearing were scaring me, noises that sounded like wolves crying and people screaming.

There it was, the shadow, it ran behind the shed. I could now see a faint person in the distance, they had a black jacket on with a black hat, black trousers and big black boots. I sat down against the wall and got my phone out to try and phone someone. I had no signal, what was I meant to do? I tried to phone the police but I didn't have time, the man had something in his hand, which looked like a knife. He was walking towards me. He started shouting at something. A dog appeared out of nowhere and started barking his head off. I had a dog, which looked exactly like that. I shouted at it. It ran toward me, it was my dog, but who was the man … ?

Samantha Neill (13)
Berwick Middle School, Berwick-upon-Tweed

He Was There But I Couldn't See Him!

I was balancing up the till at work and it was my turn to lock up. I didn't have my car so I had to walk home. I'm not a lover of the dark so I hurried through the bare streets and, as I passed the baker's, I felt someone tap my shoulder. I turned round but no one was there. I felt the cold hand touch my shoulder again so I ran home as fast as I could. I ran up the wobbly path and hugged my front door with relief. Normally when I came home late my boyfriend would be home but all the lights were off.

The living room was freezing so I turned up the heating and watched the TV. Just as I sat down the phone rang, it was my boyfriend saying he was late coming home from work. I put the phone down and went back to watching the telly. As I sat down I sat on something: it was my boyfriend's wallet but he never went anywhere without it. I went through to the bathroom before bed and I heard a noise coming from my bedroom.

When I eventually went through to bed my boyfriend's work clothes were in a heap on the floor, but he wasn't supposed to be coming home for about another hour or two. I got into bed and tried to make myself go to sleep but even counting sheep didn't work.

As I was slowly getting to sleep all the lights went off and I heard the front door slam shut ...

Amber Windram (13)
Berwick Middle School, Berwick-upon-Tweed

Afraid

I'm afraid. We were told it was safe, it wasn't. It won't ever be the same.

I'll start from the beginning. We were on holiday in Africa for Mel's wedding. It was me, Mum, Tessa and Kate going. My name is Elle. Tessa and Kate are my sisters.

Mum said it would be lovely and she was right. We were going to Kenya. I'm not sure that I want to go back now. Don't get me wrong, I had a great time but it was that one day. That one day that changed me forever.

It was after the wedding and we were staying in a house next to the sea. We were staying with Mel and one of her friends came to see us. She told us about a lovely swimming beach nearby.

So we went the next day. At first we just stayed in the shallows, as the water was cold. Then we went deeper and soon we came out because of the cold.

Then we went in again. Suddenly, Tessa shouted that she was stuck. Kate went to get her free but she got stuck as well. I went in after them. I then realised why they were stuck. It was deep and there were currents. I was getting dragged out. The waves were coming over me. I was the furthest out to sea. I managed to get hold of a rock. I was safe and I scrambled back to shore.

But what about Tessa and Kate?

Katie Joy (12)
Berwick Middle School, Berwick-upon-Tweed

Shivers

I felt my whole body shaking. Me, Sally, Liam and Craig all stared at each other. We all couldn't believe what we could see. She was small but not tiny, thin and pale. She sort of had a grin on a face, like one of those cheeky grins children give you when they've done something wrong. But what had she done? Had she done something to us? Or is that her character, cheeky and sly?

'Why are you here?' she asked in a horrible manner. I didn't like her; I don't think any of my friends liked her either. Sally started slowly walking back.

'Hey, where are you going? I'm not going to hurt you, I am only a ghost. I wish I wasn't though.' She spoke in a slow and timed voice.

'We know, we are 'cause of my big sister Ashley, she said she came here at the same age that we are now, she said you were here, you spoke to her too. Can you remember her?' Craig asked, not scared of her because he didn't believe in ghosts. I think that's why we were here; he wanted to prove to his sister that she was seeing things. I guess he was wrong. He never believes what his sister tells him, she normally tells lies to get her own way or to play a prank on Craig.

'Yes, yes I can, she has brown hair and she was small. She was with a bunch of her friends. I didn't like her. She was nasty to me,' she said. There was suddenly a silence between all of us.

Hayley Gilchrist (13)
Berwick Middle School, Berwick-upon-Tweed

The Haunted Castle

'Guess what?' Scott said quickly. 'I have heard that the castle is haunted.'

'Yeah right,' replied Lucy. 'Ghosts are not real.'

'Well … um.'

'Do you believe in ghosts?' asked Lucy.

'Well yeah do you?' Scott suspiciously asked.

'No for … um … your info.'

'News flash, news flash Lucy believes in ghosts!'

'Shut up!' cried Lucy. *'You just never shut up!'*

'What's wrong with Lucy?' asked Mrs Baboon.

'I was just talking to her,' Scott stumbled.

'Lucy what is wrong?' asked Mrs Baboon as she sat down next to her.

'It is just …' There was a pause as the bus pulled up outside the castle.

'Sorry it will just have to wait Lucy. Right OK. Now children line up in pairs outside,' cried Mrs Baboon.

Lucy was the last one to get off the bus. That was when she noticed the face in the window at the top of the castle.

'Lucy, Lucy we are going now!' shouted Scott.

'Coming,' as she ran to the end of the line.

Things kept happening and things kept moving. Voices were heard and children were going missing. One by one, only ten were left out of twenty. As they moved on Lucy noticed things that other people didn't because they were too scared, the teachers were going missing too. Then all of a sudden, there it was. The thing that Lucy saw early on at the top of the castle. People hanging in the air. What was it?

Gillian Whittle (13)
Berwick Middle School, Berwick-upon-Tweed

Moonlight

The rain poured harder against the windows and through the hole in the roof. Susan knew something was out there waiting, lurking in the shadows and in the perilous depths of the lake.

Susan woke with a start, the house was deadly quiet, no dripping from the roof, nothing. The rain must have stopped. Then came the noise of heavy breathing behind her!

Susan was too petrified to move, she lay there shaking violently. Finally, she turned to face it. Nothing. Nothing was there. But as she lit the candle and looked up to her window something was sitting on the balcony staring hungrily at her with blood-red eyes.

Susan stared back, curious. If it hadn't eaten her then, what did it want her to do? She slowly and quietly crept out of bed, slid on her shoes and opened the door.

It was freezing outside and the snow had laid a blanket on the cold ground. The huge beast leapt from the roof and galloped down the icy path. Susan followed cautiously looking around the forest as she walked. Something was watching her. The hairs on the back of her neck stood up on end.

Crack! A huge branch fell from a nearby tree, there it was staring coldly. It crept nearer, she knew this was the end. Susan closed her eyes and waited. Nothing happened. The light of the sun started to creep over the hills. She opened her eyes. The sun rose higher. Suddenly, the large beast burst into flames and ash. It had gone. Gone forever.

Emily Haddock (13)
Berwick Middle School, Berwick-upon-Tweed

Ghost In The Closet

'No one dared to get out and switch the light on. Even though that was the only thing that would make 'it' go away, the only thing that would dispel the evil that lurked into their bedroom'.

The floor started to creak. Someone was there. It was getting closer and closer. Robert and Sean were shaking with fear. Someone was at the side of their bed; it was tall and looked scary.

It lifted up the bed covers. Robert and Sean screamed with fear. 'It's only me, your mum.'

'What's all the screaming about,' said Sarah.

Sean stuttered, 'Mum ... Mum, something's in the closet!'

Sarah told them, 'Don't be so silly, it must have just been a bad dream. Goodnight boys.' As they were falling asleep they heard whispers coming from the closet. They were getting very scared again.

Robert shouted, 'Who's there?' It all went quiet. No one spoke until ... *bang!* The cupboard fell and broke as it hit the floor.

Sarah stormed in, 'What's all the noise about?' She had seen that the cupboard had fallen onto the floor. 'How did this fall over?' she said.

Robert said, 'We heard noises coming from the closet then all of a sudden it fell over.'

'I, I have had enough, go and sleep on the couch. Both of you.' They went downstairs and Robert slept on the couch and Sean slept on the airbed.

When they were trying to get to sleep they heard noises coming from the staircase. It sounded like someone was there.

Steven Colquhoun (12)
Berwick Middle School, Berwick-upon-Tweed

United In Trouble

The crowd at Exely Road were silenced when Tim Acely scored for Brockhole Rovers with only 10 minutes left, if they didn't score two goals they were relegated. Two minutes later Brockhole scored again. Exely United were relegated in the Conference South and if they didn't come up with £20,000 soon they would be kicked out of Exely Road.

A week later their top goal scorer, Jack Carson, walked out and so did the captain, Alan Fells. They were midway through selling defender Tony Ark for £12,000 but he refused the contract offered.

The owners of Exely Road gave them a deadline and it was just a week away and not a penny had been raised towards the £20,000. They had organised a friendly match against non-league team Harbour FC to try and raise funds.

The match went alright. They raised £4,000 and won 1-0 but they needed £16,000 in five days.

Disaster struck when manager Dave Calderwood walked out when he found out his contract would not be renewed at the end of the season, but to help funds he left the club £3,000.

Local league two side Grimsby Town heard about Exely's troubles and offered to have a friendly with them at Exely Road. Exely accepted the offer and although they were beaten 3-0 they had a record attendance of 2,784. They raised a whopping £10,000 but they needed £3,000 if they wanted to stay in business. With only one day to go, could they do it?

Gregor Thomson (13)
Berwick Middle School, Berwick-upon-Tweed

Beware Of The Bite

Nobody was safe. Nobody would dare go out in the dead of night because the villagers of Shillington knew what was out there, a vampire. Only one person had survived when caught outside and that was Robert. Nobody could believe that an 11-year-old boy could survive against a 700-year-old vampire. But that was years ago and Count Alan had sworn revenge on Rob now it was 2,000 and 10 years had passed.

Robert now lived with his parents since his uncle Dave had been poisoned, Robert came back. There had been shrieks of terror coming from the forest and Robert sensed Count Alan had returned and he was going to face him one more time. So getting his silver stake Robert set off into the forest.

Cautiously, Rob approached a clearing the rustling of leaves made the hair on the back of his neck stand up, he jumped as he heard the unmistakable sound of wings. Robert was sure that the count was about and he slowly made his way into the clearing then suddenly he was hit from behind with such force Rob was knocked over. He picked himself up to see Count Alan staring at him with hungry eyes. Rob knew that this was the moment that he had to finish Count Alan once and for all. So throwing himself at the count and using the silver stake he plunged it into the heart of Count Alan. The count fell to the ground and died.

Martin Hush (13)
Berwick Middle School, Berwick-upon-Tweed

Help!

Hi my name is Kerrie. I am a tall, blonde-haired skinny girl with brown eyes. We just moved from Hull to Berwick. I met this girl called Samantha from school; she came to mine for a sleepover. At the end of my estate there was a hill leading up to a really big house that looked like a mansion. And that's where it all started.

Sam said, 'Why don't we go and investigate and have a little look, oh come on, don't be a big scaredy-cat, come on!'

But I wasn't so sure. She kept calling me chicken so I had no other choice, so I eventually went.

We got ready and ran out of the door. I was scared but I didn't want to say. It was quite a long walk and we didn't speak, that made me even more nervous. I was so overwhelmed to see that the gateway to the house was blocked. I looked around for Samantha. I couldn't see her. I was really scared, then something touched my shoulder, I screamed.

'It's OK, it's only me,' said the warm, gentle voice.

I quickly turned around to see it was only Samantha fooling around. I said, 'We can't get in the gates are blocked.'

'Yes we can come and look!' Samantha said willingly.

'Look, through there, if I can fit through so can you!' said Samantha.

So I went. I got halfway through, something grabbed my leg as I looked back.

Samantha Blyth (13)
Berwick Middle School, Berwick-upon-Tweed

Enter The Lair

It's the year 3000, and the scientists from team America have travelled to the Greek island of Crete to find out about the myth of the Minotaur. The Minotaur is a half man half beast-like creature, but little did they know the Minotaur was very much alive. By this time they had the right equipment just in case.

The leader of the expedition was a person called Johnny Thunder with his right-hand man Krunk. As they made their way into the Minotaur lair they heard a loud roar coming from the centre of the labyrinth.

They were there for a week before they made it to the centre. All the team were that tired. They said, 'Let's rest for the night.'

Johnny said, 'Let's.' So after dinner they wanted to play football to celebrate the football World Cup in Mexico. The two captains were Krunk and Johnny. They put all the names of the teams in a hat and pulled out a team to play as, Krunk chose Ghana and Johnny chose Brazil.

During the night the clumsiest member of the team also known as Dopey needed the toilet, so he went to the pee bucket, when he heard something he shone his torch about then he saw three tiny little Minotaurs standing right in front of him with their hackles showing. They jumped with all their might and hit an invisible shield built by Johnny. They all went back to bed.

In the morning the team were wondering what could be the Minotaur's labyrinth.

Alan Burrow (13)
Berwick Middle School, Berwick-upon-Tweed

The Spooky Room

As I stepped on the unvarnished floorboards, I felt a cold, bony, stone-like hand on my shoulder. I jumped, there was something there I was sure of it but I wasn't certain. As I stepped, the old wooden door slammed and locked. I couldn't get out. I felt a slight draught, I thought there could be an opened window somewhere - I looked around and the only window was wedged shut. I started to panic and to my amazement there stood a tall shadow in a long black cloak draped over the shoulders of the creature. I stared at it, it looked like a tall, medium-built man but I wasn't sure.

All of a sudden a little girl appeared, she was wearing a patchwork dress and a little pair of black painted shoes with little flowers on them. She also had strawberry-blonde hair, which had been styled into ringlets. As I walked towards her she started to cry and quiver, in the corner.

'It's OK I'm here to help you, don't worry I won't hurt you I promise,' I whispered.

The little girl mumbled, 'OK, my name is Sianne and I've lost my mummy. Can you help me find her, I think she is dead. Have you seen her?'

I replied, 'No I have not seen her, what does she look like? If you like I can help you look for her, I am sure she is not dead, don't worry, OK?'

Rozie McGhee (13)
Berwick Middle School, Berwick-upon-Tweed

Multi-Storey Mall

'Welcome to the world of your dreams,' said the manager of the multi-storey mall. 'On the first floor Homes and Gardens, on the second and third floors DIY, on the fourth and fifth floors Health and Beauty, Restaurants and Cafés are on the sixth floor. Please remember sub floor parking is available and have a great time.'

'Woo hoo, let's go,' screamed Yazmin and Cloe-Louise.

'We vote Pizza Hut first,' yelled Coby and Dylan.

'Trust you to think of food,' remarked the girls.

'Well do you want to?' questioned the boys.

'Later, first let's check out the Home and Garden section, I want to get more mirrors for my room,' explained Cloe-Lou.

'OK, let's go to the Home and Garden floors, then we can go to Pizza Hut,' sighed Yazmin calmly.

'That's fine with us,' said Cloe, Coby and Dylan together, trying hard not to laugh at Yaz's calmness.

'Wow, look at all the different styles and shapes of mirrors,' dreamed Cloe. 'It's like I'm in Heaven.'

'Hurry up Clo', we're starving here,' complained Coby and Dylan.

'These go with your room so just get them,' complained Yaz quietly. 'Even I'm getting hungry.'

'OK I've got them, let's go and grab a pizza,' said Cloe hurriedly.

'One double ham and pineapple pizza please,' Yaz said.

'That will be £4.50 please,' said the cashier.

'Let's eat it here,' shouted Cloe, over the din of the loud music, playing in the restaurant.

'Mmm,' they all mumbled happily as cheese clung to their chin.

Lorna Strachan (13)
Berwick Middle School, Berwick-upon-Tweed

The Fog

Our story begins on June 4th 2006, a boy named John was coming home on the bus quietly reading his book. Nothing was different, it then all went quiet. Suddenly there was a horrific screeching noise on the side of the bus.

What was that? he thought to himself, then it happened again. He asked the bus driver to stop.

'Why stop? We are almost there.'

'No I can hear something on the side of the bus.'

All the children backed him up. The bus driver pulled over, opened the bus door and was blown away with amazement.

'Oh my!' cried the bus driver.

There were ten claw marks dragged against the side of the bus and four teeth marks imprinted into the side of the bus, everybody was stunned.

When he got home he told his parents about what happened and they were as shocked as he was. They thought that if something was going to hurt them, then maybe he should not go to school.

'I like that idea,' exclaimed John. 'We might have to see the teachers about this, and get it sorted.'

They didn't know that something was watching them from the shadows. It then slipped away back into the shadows, its face was then projected in the fog then disappeared back completely.

'Oh well fog's cleared up,' said John's mum.

After this story was written, John and eight other children disappeared on a walking exhibition, funny thing really, when you're the murderer.

Stuart Taylor (13)
Berwick Middle School, Berwick-upon-Tweed

The Pool

'Hi I'm Molly and I live in Russia. I live with my daddy; by the way we are rich as my daddy digs for oil. It was my birthday not long ago and my daddy bought me a pool.

It all started when I dived in my new pool and started to swim. The water turned rough and the waves started themselves. It was like a whirlpool. I began to go under the water. I was whirling round. I couldn't hold my breath much longer.

I woke up. I was all over the place, it looked like a swamp only, and it had a giant tree with a tiny door. I got up, walked to the door and knocked. No one answered. I went in. It was a little house. It had a kitchen and then a tiny room with a hammock. Suddenly something sharp had struck me. I felt so tired.

I woke up rubbing my leg. I pulled the dart out and more blood emerged from my sore leg. I turned around and …

I screamed, 'Argh!'

'Oh higgle grump please don't scream, we'll, we'll get caught.'

'By who?' I asked.

'The rats,' he whispered.

'What should I do?' I whispered back.

'Run before they catch you and kill you,' he mimed.

'I think I should dive in the swamp and it'll take me back.'

'Right then, now you must be leaving before we both get caught.'

I ran, the rats saw me, I dived in the swamp and …

I screamed.

'It's OK.'

'I was sitting at the side of my pool, with my dad, that was scary.'

Elvira Drummond (13)
Berwick Middle School, Berwick-upon-Tweed

The Friend He Never Knew

High up above the clouds, where the air is thin and the mist hangs over treetops, lives the lonely monk, Pei Pei. Pei Pei's home is a small monastery in peaceful surroundings, beside a calm flowing waterfall. Pei Pei is a Buddhist monk and gets up early every morning to meditate.

It was on a winter's morning, when Pei Pei awoke to the sound of the waterfall. Once he was up, he decided to go for a short walk, as he thought the mountain looked magical with snow.

So off went Pei Pei. He began at a steady pace through the trees, treading carefully so not to disturb any living thing. Pei Pei's legs weren't as strong as they used to be, so the old man sat down to rest.

'Oww!' squealed a familiar voice.

Pei Pei stood up. 'I'm terribly sorry, Zhao Meng, I seem to have sat on you. What can I do to help you, my friend?'

'Well Pei Pei, you and I have known each other for a while now, and I've come to a conclusion - you need a companion!'

'You're probably right. I have been feeling a bit lonely lately. Could you help me find a friend Zhao Meng?'

'Of course! Hop on my back and we can have a look around,' said the wise old eagle enthusiastically.

After flying round for hours, Pei Pei and Zhao Meng descended. They had found no one for Pei Pei to make friends with. The two sat quietly with a feeling of failure inside, when softly, Zhao Meng broke the silence. 'Pei Pei, what qualities did you want in your friend?'

As the old man opened his heart to the wise eagle, sharing his deepest thoughts, it slowly dawned on him that his search was over.

Anna Lannon (13)
Berwick Middle School, Berwick-upon-Tweed

Yesterday Is Today

As it sluggishly crept up to 2,000 years, past, the last missing soul in the temple of Din Yon Hoo, no man had mowed down there in a long time. It took pure utter strength and a life of experience and bravery to explore in the temple of Din Yon Hoo.

It was told that a sacred, mythical creature lived in the temple. Anyone who stumbled into the creature's tracks, were never seen again. Most visitors avoided the temple from their unfortunate hearings.

Today at this embracing morning a man named Seville - Adriano Seville. He was a young, strong, stubborn man. He was grooming up ready to take the challenge, the challenge of entering the temple of din Yon Hoo. As approaching the temple door Adriano replied, 'Gracsus iou,' which meant spare your souls. He was in the temple and taking heavy steps. He was alone with a sphere and some flares only. Adriano came to a dead end, he swivelled back and it was a dead end. He started panicking and started praying for help. He knew exactly what had happened, he had been trapped by the beast.

Everything evolved silent except from a few minor grizzle sounds. The sound enclosed on him. Suddenly, from nowhere a great mythical beast leapt out in front of him. It had long, fine gold hair; it was like half lion, half man. The beast struck him with force, Adriano attempted to protect himself but it was too late, he was gone. *Zzzz!* It seemed like the creature was too powerful for any man. Yet the secret floats away.

Elliot Wilson (13)
Berwick Middle School, Berwick-upon-Tweed

Be Careful - The Walls Will Be Listening!

'Observing. Never missing a trick. Watching. Listening. Yet never divulging. Secrets are safe with me. Walls may have ears, but we don't have mouths. Oh, but if I did, the stories I could tell, the gossip you would know. You wouldn't believe me'.

I bet you didn't know that the lady with brown hair living on Palace Street had an affair with her manager from work? I know something else, something that no one else in the whole world knows but are desperate to find out - who committed the Lesley Smith murder?

Well I know and I am dying inside because I can't tell anyone. If I could somehow open my mouth for just a few minutes, I would be able to stop the accusations and the arresting of innocent people. I would just burst and spill my guts out, if I could. I know every single detail. The time, the place, the murderer.

I watch it on the television as they condemn the wrong people and I can't do anything about it. I watch as they make guiltless people suffer while that lying malicious man is wandering the streets and free from having to spend any time paying for what he has done.

And I have to look at him every day and offer him my warmth while he sticks pins in me and makes me suffer. I have to keep his sick little secret all because I am the wall that covers his house.

Emily Elvin (13)
Berwick Middle School, Berwick-upon-Tweed

Battle Of The Bands

On a bright summer's day in his house in Santiago, Mark and his band Ninepins were practising a song for the final battle of the bands that night, they were practising 'Run to the Hills' by Iron Maiden.

There were five other bands competing. They were Inversion, 90 Below, Loose Wire, Harmonic Default and The Solution.

They had been practising for five hours straight now, so they were exhausted. 'Boys, time for tea!' shouted Mark's mum, Mark and the boys ran downstairs to see what would be waiting for them.

'Chinese!' screeched Danny.

'Mmm! My fave,' Leo said.

'Thanks Mum,' shouted Mark.

After tea Mark's mum helped them pack all their equipment into the van, it was then time to leave for the show.

On the way there they were all singing to keep themselves entertained. When the van finally pulled up outside the venue they were relieved.

The tension was rising, the curtains were being pulled up to reveal about 500 crazy rock fans shouting, screaming and moshing.

They had done it! They had survived the finals!

The judge came up to announce the winners, 'In first place, who get to make a CD and DVD of their songs, Inversion! And in second place, winning a £100 gift voucher for the music gallery, Ninepins! And finally in third place, winning £50 off at the music gallery, Loose Wire!'

When they got home they celebrated by having a party and inviting all their friends including the other bands.

Michaela Robson (13)
Berwick Middle School, Berwick-upon-Tweed

The Cottage

(An extract)

Rain fell heavily down on the forest. Amy was cold, wet and tired, although she carried on searching through the apparently deserted woods. She was determined to find her family before darkness fell and trapped her there overnight. Cautiously she dragged herself deeper into the dark and gloomy forest, often tripping over dead branches and roots on the forest floor. Then she noticed something. In the corner of her eye she could just make out a light, it was only dim but it gave Amy a last kick of hope before she reluctantly fed herself to the black woods. She had been walking for hours now and was probably kept standing only by the trees around her, but she had to get to the light.

Eventually she made it. Amy looked up, praying that she could see her little brother James, hitting Jasper, their dog, with sticks and her mum and dad running towards her with smiles spread over their faces; but that was all in her head, because as she looked up she saw before her, in the clearing, a house.

Amy tugged gently on the rotting white gate outside the old stone cottage. She was shaking, not because of the cold but because of the sheer terror sunk deep into her heart. Amy walked up to the front door, took a deep breath and stepped inside. She called quietly out to see if anyone was there.

'Hello, is anyone there? My name is Amy Morrison, I got lost in the forest, hello.' No answer came. Amy walked further into the creepy cottage - she'd die otherwise, it had to be her best hope. Or so she thought ...

Alanah McMahon (12)
Brockwell Middle School, Cramlington

The House

(An extract)

Gnarled roots of enormous trees snatched at her feet. Stumbling and shaking, she limply ventured on. Salty tears dripped silently from her frozen features leaving slimy tracks like snails do. With effort she twisted her head gingerly round, only to see that she was surrounded by more immense trees, towering high into the treacherous blanket of darkness that covered the flashing sky. Rhythmically the rain beat down remorselessly onto her lank hair. Sluggishly her head lifted upwards, searching for a sign or a whisper of evidence that would linger in her mind to give her the strength to carry on her tiresome journey. Nevertheless, as hard as her cloudy green eyes focused and as carefully as she searched the sky, no trace of civilisation was indicated in the rain-streaked canvas of the menacing sky.

Boom. The thunder sent her ears throbbing. She knew that more lightning was to follow, but intricate brambles scratched at her red-raw skin and low branches grabbed at her numb face. Although many distracting things were happening in her surroundings her mind's eye was focused on seeking hope in a place where there was none. In a split second of sheer luck or perhaps peril, a blinding fork of lightning struck a gigantic oak tree sending it bursting into colourful flames. Her face lit up and a wild grin set like stone on her radiant face. The flames flickered and danced and plumes of hazy smoke drifted elegantly up, being singed by the heavy downpour on its way. But it was not the flames that she was staring so contented at, as her glazed-over stare was concentrated on something more distant. Covered thickly by climbing green ivy and belittled by vibrant bluebells and long shoots of wild grass, moss scattered the pale grey walls. But this did not matter for although the house was ramshackle it looked small and almost cosy. Ancient red roof slates on the brink of falling off round windows cracked and filthy and a distinctive bronze door-knocker with the peculiar profile of a wolf's head. It would at least provide some shelter in such a daunting and incognito location. Slowly the gate creaked open.

She stumbled into the dense maze of entangled flowers and anonymous wild grasses. She trod cautiously upon the fungi-choked path that squelched under the extensive strain of her weight, like a sponge being compressed. Thoughts of anxiety tugged at her mind, screaming out to her to consider the consequences of entering the mysterious habitation, so alone in these misleading and perilous woods like yellow jacket amongst many purple. She ignored these thoughts and shunted them out like a lonesome candle starved of oxygen as she knew there was no going back as the storm still raged. The lightning illuminated the crooked house, putting it in an eerie perspective. Later she found out ignoring these thoughts was to be the biggest mistake of her life.

Sophie Coyle (12)
Brockwell Middle School, Cramlington

Untitled

Hello my name is Thomas Armstrong. I am about to tell you the terrifying experiences of World War II.

I was 19 years old. I lived in a small cottage in Durham. I had just come back from mining. My face had turned black with coal. I sat down for supper with my brother, Michael and my mum when a deep-voiced man announced something that had shocked us all. 'Attention listeners, I have some shocking news, World War II has been declared! There will be some British troops marching round each town tomorrow night at 6pm. All men over the age of 17 will go to war.'

My heart had pounded so much I thought it would explode. I suddenly burst into tears lying on the table. No one said a world, not even Michael who always said things to calm me down. I was thinking that I would be by myself without my mum and Michael. I wish Michael could come but he is only 16. We were all so lost in the moment that Mum and I nearly fell off our chairs. Michael told us that maybe he could pretend to be 17 and go to the war with me. Michael had never let me down. Mum started yelling at Michael telling him war isn't just a game, it is a life-losing experience.

I remembered that night I couldn't get to sleep. I was too scared in case our house got bombed.

The dreaded next day had come. We all had the day off at the pits for the troops announcing the men who would go to war. Nearly the entire town was lined up facing each other. The troops marched up the street in their uniforms and polished boots. After about an hour I was back at home crying and so was my mum. I had been chosen to be in the war. I left the morning after. My suitcases were packed. My new boots were sparkling. And Michael just sat on his bed staring at the wall.

There is one thing I still don't get about what Michael did. Why did he go with me to the world war where there is death lurking around every corner?

We set off in the morning saying goodbye to Mum and waved to all the townspeople. On the train it smelt really bad like thousands of cigarettes. We made loads of stops until we eventually got to London where we got shipped to France.

We saw the German trenches, they were so dark and misty, it looked like a deserted mansion. At that time it was about 3.30am. We were all thinking how on earth we were going to beat these people, considering we had never used a gun in our lives. About half an hour had passed, everything went so quiet. Then we heard from silence to screaming of pain, already about 10 of our men had been killed. Me and Michael grabbed our guns and fired away at the Germans who had sneaked over our fences.

The sound of gunfire was like going to Hell. I thought my ears would explode. I can't wait for this to end ...

Alex Newman (11)
Brockwell Middle School, Cramlington

Creek Wood House

(An extract)

Alone, lost and exhausted, Caz stumbled over the wreckage of a decaying oak tree, feet sinking into the saturated earth. The rain was cascading down from the dark, menacing sky with the force of a waterfall, and the occasional drum-like rumble of thunder echoed through the perished forest. Deadly, sharply-jagged forks of lightning pierced the cold atmosphere, always bearing the possible threat of striking a tree and setting it alight. All of these tantalising matters added to the heavy burden of stress that was weighing Caz down.

Easing her way through the brambles, she nervously looked around, and from the barren animal burrows, Caz found no evidence or indication of any civilised form of life throughout the hollow forest; she found this extremely unnerving. Her shaking hand reached and touched her throbbing bloodstained head, transferring a pattern of pure red blood to her hand - the unfortunate result of the trying events that had occurred previously that evening. Another sharp fork of lightning flashed, illuminating the silhouette of a crooked house for a split second, only to cover it again with a sheet of bewilderment and darkness, Caz noticing it, clambered wearily towards it.

Breathing heavily she staggered to stand at the foot of the large severely dilapidated house with its quirky, antiquated features. She limped round the perimeter of the grand old building, carefully observing the state of this intimidating mansion. She then came to the eroding, cobwebbed front door, the porch floor was strewn with sopping newspapers, and a mouldy doormat stubbornly lay on the unstable wood. She cautiously knocked ... no answer or noise could be heard. She paused and peered through the rusty letter box, it was too dark to make out any objects, but she was positive she had seen a flicker of movement glide across, what she assumed, was the hall.

'Hello is anyone home?' No reply, she listened carefully, but nothing would be heard over the worsening eruptions of thunder. A glimmer of shining marble caught her eye, wiping away the rain and dirt that had splattered it, it revealed in gold letters the words *Creek Wood House*. Aching and tired, and unable to sustain the simple task of standing much longer, Caz placed her bony hand on the icy door handle and pushed effortlessly. *Click!* Creaking eerily the ancient door swung open ...

Jessica Morris (12)
Brockwell Middle School, Cramlington

How The Tiger Got Its Stripes

One warm, sunny afternoon Tasha the tiger was doing her chores as normal. Now Tasha was the prettiest tiger in all of Asia. Her fur glowed as brightly as the sun. Her eyes shone like crystals with deep pools of oil set in the centre of them. Her fur was as soft as the early morning mist. She moved as smoothly as silk flowing along my neck.

While Tasha was out in the field the farmer called, 'Tasha come here.'

She ran as fast as she could towards the farmer. Was this the glorious day that the farmer would give her back her freedom? It was. The farmers, so that they could keep track of the released tigers, had to burn her beautiful coat. She left with a morning mist soft coat but with horrendous black stripes, which has now become a thing of beauty.

That is how the tiger got its stripes but at least it gives tigers, these days, their freedom.

Lindsay Ibbetson (12)
Dallam School, Milnthorpe

How The Lion Got Its Mane

Around 50 years ago there was a lion called Leo who lived with his family on a deserted plain in Africa. Leo had soft golden fur and light blue eyes. One day Leo was out hunting for his dinner when he heard footsteps. Leo had never heard this noise before as it was only his family which lived on the African plain. So he took no notice and carried on looking for something to eat. A few minutes later a vicious hunter appeared in front of Leo. Leo was so scared he ran as fast as he could towards the spiky bushes. He wanted to stop but the ground was slippy and sandy. He was heading right for the spiky bushes.

Leo slid into the bushes and got all his fur caught on the branches. When Leo tried to move his fur got more tangled and matted. Finally he was able to pull his fur away from the spiky bushes. He came face to face with the hunter. But Leo looked so scary the hunter ran away. After this lions were born with fluffy manes. That is how the lion got its mane.

Georgia Pritchard (12)
Dallam School, Milnthorpe

How The Elephant Got Its Trunk

Now I am going to tell you the story of how the elephant got its long trunk, as years ago elephants had stubby noses and so here's the story of how the elephant got its long trunk.

It all started one scorching day in the African jungle, there lived a mischievous baby elephant called Jordan. He never did what his mum and dad told him to do. As you can guess they were very fed up with him. As they could not control him.

One sunny morning Jordan woke up early and sneaked off before his parents woke up. He ran down to the lake and jumped in with an almighty splash, though making the big mistake of Mr Snap the crocodile.

'Oh sorry Mr Snap, *not!*' shouted Jordan, rudely.

'Don't worry little kiddie,' mumbled Mr Snap, with a sly grin spread across his face.

'Haha! As if I am worried about you,' sniggered Jordan, feeling very proud of himself for being so rude.

'Well do you want me to tell you a really big secret,' said Mr Snap, chuckling to himself.

'Oh yes yes do!' said Jordan the elephant.

'Well come closer then,' said Mr Snap.

So Jordan the elephant slowly leaned forward to hear Mr Snap's very big secret, but when he got to Mr Snap's big jaw he grabbed Jordan's stubby trunk. In pain Jordan tried to wriggle free from Mr Snap's mouth, but his stubby nose ended up stretching into a long trunk. And so that's how the elephant got its long trunk.

Jenna Taylor (12)
Dallam School, Milnthorpe

How The Kangaroo Got His Bounce

There was once a kangaroo called Oswald and an elephant called Kudrow. They both were best friends, so they decided to go on a walk in the woods. On their way around, they saw a squirrel jumping up and down at the nearest tree.

'What are you doing?' Oswald asked.

'Well, my nut I bought got stuck in the tree and I can't get it down!' the squirrel answered.

'How on earth did you get that stuck up there?' Kudrow wondered.

'I was minding my own business and Mr Mean Giraffe took it off me and put it in the tree!' the squirrel moaned.

'You poor little thing, let us help you,' smiled Oswald.

'Thank you. Maybe you could jump and get it down?'

'Well I don't think I can jump very well, but I will give it a go!' Oswald mentioned. 'OK, here goes.' Oswald jumped up high and reached the nut!

'Wow, you're a really brilliant jumper!'

'Oh, thank you!'

'You're welcome,' the squirrel said.

'I never thought I could jump!' Oswald was so pleased with his new talent he jumped everywhere, and that is how the kangaroo got its bounce.

Anna Wieclawska (12)
Dallam School, Milnthorpe

How Did The Elephant Get Its Long Trunk?

One day, a little baby elephant was trying to reach some leaves in a big tree. But he couldn't reach with his little trunk. Just then, there was a loud bang and men were after him and the other elephants. The little baby elephant couldn't run fast, so he was left behind. He stumbled on a tree root and it wrapped around his ankle. When the men got to him they tried to pull him out by using his trunk. But instead of pulling him out, they made his trunk long and stretched, so they left him to starve.

Now the little elephant had a long trunk, he snapped the root with it and went to the herd to show off his trunk.

Daniel Simpson (11)
Dallam School, Milnthorpe

How The Panda Got Its Patches

One day Piper the panda was eating bamboo and he heard a noise. It was a splashing noise, but he just ignored it and carried on eating his bamboo.

The next day he heard the splashing noise again, so he put his bamboo stick down and went off to investigate. The noise got louder and louder as he got closer and closer, He came to a lagoon, it was pitch-black in colour and all the elephants were having a water fight.

'Please can I join in?' Piper asked.

'No, you're too small, go play with the monkeys,' the elephants replied and gave Piper a big splash, and the black water left big black splodges on him. So that is how the panda got its patches.

Justine Walker (12)
Dallam School, Milnthorpe

How The Kangaroo Got Its Hop

One beautiful day a kangaroo, called Skippy, wished that he could hop instead of walk, because he was getting older and he couldn't afford anymore walking shoes. He told his friend Henry, the hyena, about his little crisis. So he scratched his head and wrenched out a dazzling pair of shiny gold springs.

'What are they for?' Skippy asked curiously.

'What does it look like? They're springs which I'm going to ram onto your feet, OK?'

'You'd better be careful or I'll be having you for dinner.'

So Henry rammed the golden dazzlers up into Skippy's feet, and that was that. So now Skippy was happy, and he was better off from not buying all those walking shoes. And that is how the kangaroo got its hop.

Joe Laisby (12)
Dallam School, Milnthorpe

How The Mouse Got Its Squeak

One beautiful day in August when the sun was shining and the birds were singing, Tilly, the mouse, was playing in a garden. Tilly loved the summer, especially at the end of the summer when it was harvest time and she would roam about in the fields of wheat and nibble on it.

Tilly was just playing in a garden, when the owners of the garden came out of the house next to it. They came out with a baby too. The baby sat happily in her pram and Tilly didn't think much of this, so carried on playing while the baby's parents went back inside.

As Tilly was playing, she didn't notice that she was getting closer to the baby and fell over the baby's foot. The baby jumped, started crying and dropped her squeaking pig on the floor. The pig broke and the squeaker flew into the air. Tilly was in such shock her mouth was wide open and the small squeaker fell right into her mouth and down her throat. Tilly squeaked with her new squeaker and ran away.

That is how the mouse got its squeak!

Eleanor Peach (12)
Dallam School, Milnthorpe

New Girl

'Come on, girls, I need this place spotless. She'll be here soon,' Jenny shouted. Jenny was tall, blonde-haired and very kind and helpful. They were trying to get the yard spotless because there was a new girl coming and they wanted to make a good impression.

'She's here,' one of the girls hollered.

So they quickly put their stuff away and lined up as this big white wagon pulled through the gate with windows that you could see out of but you couldn't see through. The wagon came to a halt, the door opened and this tall girl with brown hair came out and walked over to Jenny.

'Hi, Sam, how are you? Welcome to High Tree Meadows Farm, please step this way and we will introduce you to everyone,' Jenny said.

'OK,' she replied.

A couple of minutes later, the had been all the way down the line and all of the girls were saying, 'Get your horse out, get your horse out, please.'

'OK,' Sam said. So she walked round the back and pulled the back down and this tall black figure was standing there. Sam walked in and brought him out so everyone could stroke him and then she led him to his new stable so he could settle down. As for Sam, she settled down quite quickly as well.

Lauren Moffatt (12)
Ormesby School, Middlesbrough

Cyprus In The Sun

As I look around I can see the golden sun setting behind the red and orange clouds. It is a lovely sight. I can hear the sweet sound of the ice cream van. I can see a flake ice cream as the cold vanilla runs down my hands. I can smell the chocolate melting, melting in the heat. I can hear the sweet waves rushing and rolling on the warm sand. I can feel the warm sand rushing through my toes.

As the day grows old, I think my chance to take a dip has gone. But no, it hasn't. I go for a dip, then I go to my hotel room. I get changed and read a relaxing book.

Nicole Elrick (12)
Ormesby School, Middlesbrough

Lost In The Woods

One dark and dingy night there was a group of people lost in the woods. The trees were whistling in the wind and it was raining. They all felt cold and terrified. Suddenly, one started to sink in quicksand. They all started to run, screaming their heads off.

They came to a boarded up house. They went in. There was a settee and the boy sat on it, and the settee ate him! The other people tried to save him.

The door slammed shut and day after day, each one died.

Mark Blowers (11)
Ormesby School, Middlesbrough

The Night Of The Unexpected

The wind was howling through the trees at the side of the road. When the wind blew stronger, it sounded almost like a scream. The clouds were heavy and black, but the wind had no problem pushing them across the night sky. The only light was that of the full moon and only then when allowed by the breaks in the clouds.

The trees creaked and groaned under the strength of the wind; the leaves rustled and swirled around my legs and feet. In the distance a dog barked, or it was a howl. In front of me I could see two small lights that seemed to be moving towards me slowly. In the pitch-dark of the night, the rain started to become heavier and hurting, driven by the strong, unforgiving, invisible wind.

The two small lights flickered in the distance but it was hard to tell in the driving rain. The rain was icy cold and stinging my hand and face and head. The wind was howling like a thousand wolves. The rain was hitting like a thousand small darts. The sound was getting louder and the rain was getting harder and the two small lights were getting bigger and brighter. A flash of lightning lit up the night sky, the thunder crashed and the two bright lights stopped and hovered silently in front of me. With all the noise of the storm, I never heard or saw the man get out of the large van. It was only when he walked into the beam of the headlights that I could see he was tall and broad, and had huge strong hands. He approached slowly with long, heavy strides. He reached under the big, heavy overcoat and pulled out his identity card and said, 'Good evening, Madam, I'm Dave from Roadside Recovery. Let's see if we can get you on your way.' He reached back inside his coat and pulled out the long, sharp knife.

The last thing I remember was a sharp pain across my throat and the sound of gurgling, and then everything went black. I felt numb. I was on my way, all right ... to the other side.

Laura-Mae Newton (12)
Ormesby School, Middlesbrough

Death At Your Door

The fog was thick, the moon was dull and danger laid everywhere. In the distance a glimmer of light appeared, my next victim. The time for her was now.

My scythe still dripping. The blood trickling down my arm, still warm. My cloak hid me in the night sky, it hides me from everything and everyone. As I moved forward the long green grass scraped my bony legs, I did not notice then. I was too focused on the matter at hand.

My method was flawless, practise really does make perfect. I stalk my victims like a lion with a zebra. It is only a matter of time until I strike. As I crept towards the light something happened that I did not foresee. I stumbled into an abandoned quarry. The perfect place for a silent kill.

The silent hills stood strong all around me and, worst of all, the light had gone. I must find it again. What could I do to get their attention? My only option was to hurt myself. Hurt myself so much that the pain would make me scream.

I took my blade and placed it across my arm. I sucked in lots of air, scrunched my eyes shut and pulled as hard as I could. The pain was unbelievable, a scream came bellowing out of my vocal chords, which echoed all around the hills. Surely she must have heard it. I waited and waited. Then there she was. Time for the fun to begin.

Rob Hunter (14)
Park View Community School, Chester-le-Street

Castle Athuned

'Janet come on. It's freezing and you're shivering.'

Janet reluctantly went into the abandoned castle. Inside it was dark and eerie, calm and quiet, until ... *crash!*

Janet and Drew both jumped.

'Where did that come from?' Drew asked now, shivering. 'Hello? Hello? No one's there, it's fine. Probably just the wind.'

Janet still wasn't convinced. 'Let's go upstairs, see what's up there.'

As Janet was walking up the stairs, in front of Drew, she began to get scared. Drew mumbled something, which Janet didn't hear. But when she turned around, Drew wasn't there.

Screaming for Drew, Janet ran to the front door. The door was locked, Janet backed up, dialling 999. 'Hello, hello I'm tra ...' The phone went dead.

Janet tried to find somewhere to hide, until it got light, but everywhere she went she got the feeling someone was watching her.

Standing beside the window, she saw car lights going past. She banged on the window screaming. But nothing. They just drove straight past. Something wasn't right about this castle.

Crash! Janet spun around, faster than the noise had even finished. All she could see were chairs, tables and dead flowers. Something was coming towards her. She could sense it. She screamed and screamed but she realised no one was coming to save her.

By the time the police traced the call, some two hours later, the castle was again eerie, calm and quiet.

One police officer stepped in the door and saw blood everywhere. He looked up and saw, hanging from the ceiling was one man and one woman.

Charlotte Bell (14)
Park View Community School, Chester-le-Street

Diary Of Sally Ringland

10th May

Today was the worst day ever! All my friends are falling out and they have all been talking about me behind my back! I'm so angry! *And* when I try to talk to my mam about these things she just says, 'Oh well that's life,' which doesn't help at all! When I woke up this morning I had a *huge* spot! And I found out I'm failing at school! Ah man! Anything else want to go wrong!

11th May

Could life get any worse! The most embarrassing thing ever happened today! I was walking down the stairs to the front of assembly in front of the whole of my year when I tripped over my lace and fell flat on my face! Everybody burst out laughing! Including Arron Smith, the most adorable, loveable, cutest boy ever! Embarrassment or what! Mam reckons it will all be forgotten about by tomorrow but it won't! It's going to haunt the rest of my school life! Total embarrassment!

13th May

Sorry I didn't write yesterday. I was out with Arron Smith! Yes that's right *Arron Smith!* The most adorable, loveable, cutest boy ever that I've fancied for years! He asked me out yesterday and we went to the cinema last night! All my friends have made up now and everything is fine! I'm *so so sooo* happy! How could life go from being so bad to so good! Oh well that's life!

Abby Knox (14)
Park View Community School, Chester-le-Street

The Life!

Life, isn't it a wonderful thing. Some people can bear to say, 'Oh, I hate life.' They mustn't mean it because really, there is nothing more special than life itself. But what is the perfect life? I tell you what it is … it's being a cat!

My name is Joey and I am nearly two years old. I was bought from a strange place when I was around six months old. It was a horrible little place, really smelly! I lived there for a while with my two brothers. They used to spend all day fighting and playing while I slept or watched them just keeping out of it. I wasn't very active at the time you see. But anyway after six months I was taken away by these onlookers. They watched me relax with smiles on their faces. I felt so happy and I felt like I wanted to go and jump into their arms.

After I'd got to my new home I felt a bit upset, I missed my mother. I cried for a while but eventually I stopped. The woman that bought me picked me up and held me very close, stroking me softly. I began to purr rapidly. I felt like finally I was back at home. Later on I met the whole family and I became accustomed to the house.

The rest of the one and a half years became a dream. Sleep, eat, run outside in the sun, lie around wherever you want. You see … what I'm trying to say is … this is … *the life!*

Peter Spence (14)
Park View Community School, Chester-le-Street

My 13th Birthday

Tuesday 9th May

Went to visit Grandad today. The doctors say he's got only seven days to live and that's the maximum. I hope he lives for my birthday on Thursday. In his days he used to be a keen biker rider, the fastest rider in the Shrewsbury Hill bike marathon to be exact. He taught me how to ride my own bike when I was five. We were going to watch the bike races on TV like old times. But now I don't think he'll get the chance.

Wednesday 10th May

Grandad died today. I'm sleeping in the hospital because I wouldn't leave when Mum tried to take me home. It's really upsetting but everyone has to go at some time. He died during the night and I didn't even have the chance to say goodbye. I'm too sad to talk.

Thursday 11th May

It's my birthday today, although I don't feel like celebrating much. I opened my presents, but came straight back upstairs. I've been looking at photos of my grandad. I think I'm going to go to the tree house.

I went to the tree house to find a present from my grandad. It was the picture of me and him when he taught me to ride a bike, framed in a frame we'd made together. He also left a note saying: 'Just a little something from me to you. I love you very much and will always watch over you and come to visit you although you may not notice me'.

Kane Daglish (13)
Park View Community School, Chester-le-Street

Untitled

I'm not sure how long I've been in this room, nor am I sure how long I will be here. I have no idea where I am or what these people want from me. The only thing I do know is that they are watching me. Constantly. They can see my every move, my every attempt to escape. I just hope the camera can't pick up sound as well. I don't want them to be able to hear my agonising screams of pain. I wouldn't want to give them that satisfaction.

I've probably been here only a couple of days but my insides are already aching from hunger. I remember waking up here. Alone. Frightened. Confused. Desperate. I guess now I'm starting to get used to it. I think there is something in here, some form of gas that is slowly killing me because since I got here I've been coughing up blood and I'm definitely becoming weaker.

I don't even know why I'm writing this. The monsters who are watching me will probably find it and laugh at my suffering. I guess I just have some hope that someone else will come along and find this. Come and find me. Maybe even find the sick people who are doing this to me. The people who are leaving me to rot. The people who are torturing me and don't give it a second thought. The people that are watching me die.

Sarah Elliott (14)
Park View Community School, Chester-le-Street

Little Red Dot

Fear comes in many different ways. But not as horrid nor thrilling as what Richard Crawsdale was about to experience. It was an early Sunday morning, the sun beamed into the crowds of eager New Yorkers prowling the market. Crawsdale was a normal man. His cream tweed jacket blew in the breeze as he attempted to weave his way through the masses of people. Richard found an exit and made his way onto the pathway. Crime was everywhere; closer than he thought.

A scream. A man was sprinting, clearing the shocked public off the sidewalk. He couldn't understand. Why were they afraid? Then he saw it. It reflected in the sunlight; the stranger waved it round like a stick; almost as if it wasn't a silver-plated handgun. The paths had emptied. The figure stopped directly in front of a trembling Crawdale - huddled on the nearby wall. The man looked around for an exit, anywhere to hide or run. Uniformed men swarmed in, taking cover behind cars or walls.

Richard abruptly felt the cold silencer being thrust into the back of his neck. He quickly followed the man's order to rise before being violently held around his neck; still with the weapon aimed at his head. It appeared out of nowhere. A small red dot started to move along the floor. It crawled up the villain's leg like a bug. The spot moved upwards before settling on the crook's forehead. His anxious eyes closed, certain he'd heard, 'Take him out.'

Nick Spencer (14)
Park View Community School, Chester-le-Street

Taking Over The Land

You have left me but I can sense your presence growing stronger, growing bolder!

It was a spring evening, the infernal sun was gently setting in the peachy sky, engulfed by fluffy white clouds like lambs' coats. The sun was so bright it seemed to burst from the sky and come down to Earth like a meteorite from Heaven, its radiant shafts gently sweeping the dunes.

A young girl was standing on the cliff watching the world go by. A vibrant golden sheet of hair flowing like a river of molten gold and in the soft tranquillising spring breeze. Her eyes were bright green like dazzling emeralds as they sparkled like the sea below, with never-ending black curly lashes.

Another girl was hatching a plot, a plot which could turn milk sour, her flaming wavy hair lighting an eerie dark room. She was creating poison, a cocktail of death for even the toughest of people. She travelled from the dark world of her own to the radiant world of the princess, hoping to take over. She stopped to put her poison in her pocket.

She finally reached her destination, a cliff, reached for her poison and poured it onto the lush green grass and turned it acidic green. The unaware princes stared into the sunset, captivated as the poison seeped through her, turning every thought black. The princess arose with every thought poisoned by suicide, jumped off the cliff and smacked to the ground, crimson blood scattered the sand.

Jane Gibbon (13)
Park View Community School, Chester-le-Street

The Mirror

7th May 2006

I've been living here for five months now and it's starting to feel like home. I still miss London and my friends but I'm settling in. I've had to adjust, and that wasn't easy. A different country; a different family and different weather. That's the only thing I like about California. I just wish the sun came to London.

For a while now strange things have been happening; ever since I bought that mirror. When I look in it to do my hair, I see a shadow behind me. When I turn around there's nothing there. Things have been disappearing as well. My hairbrush, my favourite top. Mam and Dave say they haven't seen them and my stepbrothers haven't taken them.

10th May 2006

I woke up in the night and saw someone standing over me with a knife. I thought it was just my imagination, but all this other stuff's been happening. I opened the cupboard and a bowling ball would've landed on my head if I hadn't seen it. In the kitchen I slipped and would've cracked my head open if Jake hadn't caught me.

11th May 2006

The bowling ball that nearly fell on me has nearly killed Kyle. I'm sure it was meant for me. I was watching television when I heard a thud. I went upstairs and found Kyle, unconscious, on my bedroom floor. The ambulance has just taken him away.

It's that mirror. No one's safe while it's around.

Alex Thompson (13)
Park View Community School, Chester-le-Street

Car Crash

The hour was late and driving while drowsy is not the most sensible thing to do. I had just been at a party held after work and despite the fact that I was tipsy I had to drive home now I was in the middle of the countryside and completely lost.

The fog was rolling over the hills and the darkness devoured my silver car as I drove on. Sleep was actually getting the better of me and I do not know whether I was hallucinating or not but I was certain I'd spotted something strange.

A white silhouette of a woman suspiciously hurried along the road about fifty yards ahead. My heart leapt and I slammed on the brakes. The car began to skid and slide but I would easily hit the person.

But this is what surprised me. The woman passed straight through the windscreen and through me. I screamed as an ice-cold chill froze my insides. I looked at the side mirror only to see that the figure had vanished without noticing I'd driven through her.

The road was as slippery as ever and my car swerved way out of control. My seconds were limited until the oncoming lorry crashed into me. Then there was more dark than the night itself.

But then I felt full of life and was able to move as freely as ever. It seemed as though I was nothing. I had no weight and couldn't touch myself. However I was back in the same place as before. Furthermore once again I had the fright of my life as another car came speeding towards me. I stood there, too petrified to move and the car hurtled straight through me.

I have to say it hurt me more the time I was in a car accident.

Nicholas Blaszczyszyn (14)
Park View Community School, Chester-le-Street

The Diary Of Tillulah Penniwinkle Aged 14 And One Eighth

Hello, I'm Tillulah Penniwinkle, 14 and one eighth.

7th May 2006

Dear Diary,

Today was an eventful day in Apple Bay Terrace. It started off just a normal day and I went to school with my friends. When I got home, I went outside with my friends, Tashie, Phillipe, Ogge and Adem. We decided to go into the woods for a walk, we had to clamber over rivers and climb over fences. We reached a point where we had been before except this time we decided to keep walking and see where we would end up. We kept walking and walking, but then my trousers ripped! Everyone found it funny and to hide my embarrassment I laughed as well.

We carried on climbing over rivers, up trees and on stepping stones. Phillipe got stuck in the mud and I found it hilarious! Anyway, we kept on going and when we eventually thought we were near home we discovered that we were on private land so we had to keep walking! We were lost!

We eventually saw a pathway to a field we followed and soon realised we were at a dual carriageway two miles from home. I looked at my watch only to find I was already 10 minutes late. The only thing we could do was keep walking, to try and get home as quickly as possible. We did it, we ended up home 45 minutes late (complete knee-high in mud). I'm tired from all that walking! Goodnight!

Julia Steele (13)
Park View Community School, Chester-le-Street

Back For Revenge

Matt Tuck strode onto the stage. Crowds cheered, cameras flashed, a buzz of happiness and excitement filled the air. The atmosphere was amazing!

'We are 'Bullet For My Valentine' from South Wales! Glad to be here child,' echoed Matt's voice.

The crowd screamed. The music began. Bullet For My Valentine's first World Tour had really taken off.

Twenty minutes into the concert Matt shouted, 'This one's called 'All These Things I Hate'!

The opening rift began. Suddenly the lights flicked off, the music came to a sudden halt and the crowd began to chant.

'I'm back. Back for revenge just like I warned you all those years ago,' whispered an angry voice in Matt's ear.

'Zacky! No! Not tonight, please!' replied a shocked Matt.

'Yes tonight. Perfect. You're not doing too bad for yourself are you my old friend? Touring the world with my band!' Zacky grimaced as he clasped his hands around Matt's throat.

'I'm sorry! Please! I'll do anything!' struggled Matt.

'Don't scream. They can't hear you anyway,' Zacky soothed.

Struggling for breath Matt tried to scream for help.

'I said don't scream!' Zacky tightened his grip around Matt's throat, looked in his eyes and hissed, 'You ruined me Matt. I was left with nothing while you got the money rolling in!'

'I ... sorry ...'

'Sorry just doesn't cut it!' and with that Matt was gone.

'Vengeance by name vengeance by nature!' cackled Zacky as he ran for the exit ...

Sarah Haswell (14)
Park View Community School, Chester-le-Street

In This Life Or The Next?

Dear Susie,

We have been married now for five years and I can't but sense that the end is edging closer like the elongating shadows as the day goes on. Too many times have I been spared from death! Too many times have I been saved by a fellow comrade taking my bullet! The brass bullet which was destined to send me to those pearly gates. Too many times I have pick-pocketed the life of others but have robbed death from consuming me!

Every day I am subject to lice and rats mauling me, thriving on my flesh, after all it's survival of the fittest. The Germans plague us with gas attacks, choking people who should've died hereafter. I am haunted by the heavy artillery bombardments raining upon our trench and obscuring my vision like a thick blanket of fog.

Helmets placed over vertically - embedded rifles signal the final resting place of those killed, sending a reminder to all. Although tomorrow I'm going 'over the top', hoping to storm the German fortifications. If this is the last letter you receive, you will know why! I love you so much that I cannot put it into words. I will always be watching over you and will meet you again in this world or the next. You will find love again, don't deny yourself. Find consolation in the fact that my experience with these men fighting for you and the country I love so was once in a life.

All my love … Jamie.

Jamie French (14)
Park View Community School, Chester-le-Street

Exam Like No Other

Before Kisa knew what was happening she was standing on top of a mountain looking out on the doll-town below. Her mum's 'keep your chest warm' attitude meant she had been coerced into wearing two jumpers, so she felt somewhat like a walking muffin. It was the SIS entrance test, notoriously scary and hard to pass. A towering sergeant strutted over to her, brandishing a harness. He roughly strapped Kisa up, and told her to run on his command. 'What?' she questioned. 'You want me to run off the edge of a cliff?'

He laughed at her, 'You'll figure it out, go!' he shouted.

Kisa closed her eyes and sprinted for all her life was worth, her legs motoring below her, she looked down and realised she was no longer on the cliff, but she was running through thin air. Thinking quickly, she pulled the cord attached to her harness and a paraglide chute bloomed from her backpack. Eyes bulging, the landscape below took her breath away - the feeling of the rushing wind tickling her cheeks. She sounded like a fighter jet as she screamed every time she swooped and dived. The ground below neared and Kisa's heart raced, with a final thud she landed on the soft grass and her test was over as quickly as it had started.

The colonel walked over to her, an unreadable expression on his face - Kisa was shaking in anticipation.

'Well done,' he announced. 'Welcome to the SIS.'

Charlotte Marlow (13)
Park View Community School, Chester-le-Street

Grumpy Old Billy

Once upon a time, there was a 'grumpy' old man called Billy, and he was sick of life as he never did anything except eat, sleep and pout. One day, some teenagers were hanging around outside his house. Billy ignored them. But then, 10 minutes later, there was a thudding sound at the window, Billy kept ignoring. Suddenly, there was a *crash!* This time, Billy looked and a stone went through the window. So Billy went outside and tried to chase them away, but when he ran across the road to get them, there was a car coming and, not seeing Billy, he ran him over.

Grumpy old Billy was in terrible pain and taken into hospital immediately. There were no injuries except for one broken ankle, which was tended to straight away. He had to stay in hospital for a week and being the grumpy person he is, he had nobody to watch his house during his absence.

At the hospital, they gave Billy anything he needed and it was then, he began to change. He started to feel kindness, love and happiness, but it was not to last. On his final day in hospital, the teenagers returned and they weren't exactly happy. So to show their hatred, they stuck a lit match through the letter box and ran. The flames grew and grew until the house had completely burned down. Billy got home to find his house gone. All the kindness left and he was 'grumpy' old Billy once again.

Nicholas Langford (13)
Park View Community School, Chester-le-Street

The Loot

I awoke not knowing what time it was. My head, banging, thumping, a chilling coldness ran down my neck. Beginning to rise sharp pains shot down my back as I realised that the chilling coldness was blood dripping down my head. Confused, wondering how I came to be in this state, I looked around noticing that strangely I was in a street, thinking, *where am I?* I rubbed the mixture of broken glass combined with rubble off my clothes.

Searching the streets I began to feel like I'd been here before and everything seemed familiar. Still full of mystery I noticed the strange quietness, the shops were deserted. In disbelief I called for someone, anyone. 'Hello,' I called, but hopelessly the only replies were the continuous echoes. Slightly startled by the idea of a ghost town I slowly made my way towards SEP, a nearby electronic store, in search for a sign of life.

As I approached the shop window I noticed a light. Tiptoeing, cautiously, in case of a dangerous stranger, I noticed that the light was beaming from a television screen. The screen appeared to be frozen on IBF News Station. A news flash warning of a nuclear attack big enough to destroy the world was the frozen image on the screen. It sounds bizarre yet this image appeared familiar.

I began to remember something, something violent. A loot. The whole town began to loot, why? Things turned violent, I got hit over the head with a glass bottle then …

Craig Loughlin (14)
Park View Community School, Chester-le-Street

The Stalking Of The Living And The Hunting Of The Dead

Huh! Audrey gasped as she sat bolt upright in her bed, her nightdress sticking to her sweaty back, another dream ... another *bad* dream!

She lay back down slowly and sunk her head into the soft, cushiony pillow as she tried to retain her breath. She stared up at the ceiling in despair. She'd never had a recurring dream before but this one seemed to be getting out of hand! Her husband Gary, had been awoken at the same ridiculous hour every night for the past week or so now, due to the constant tossing and turning of his wife as she lay restlessly beside him. This very inconvenient situation had begun the previous Tuesday, late on in the afternoon ...

Audrey had been in the kitchen fetching her watering can, in order to water the dry, sun-baked plants in the back garden. When, as she was filling it up, she noticed a reflection on the base of the sink. To start with it was blurry, hard to make out. However as Audrey focused her mind, it became noticeably clearer. It was a face! She didn't recognise this face, but when she looked closely at it, it appeared to be quite vivid and she soon realised that its powerful gaze was fixed on her very own eyes! Her scream was piercing and flooded the entire house! What was this?

So, over the next few days, Audrey became noticeably more conscious of her surroundings, and started seeing blurry, steam-like images in mirrors and on walls etc ... By the time Sunday arrived she was paranoid! Ghostly noises crept eerily around the house at night and spooky shadows floated through rooms. Doors started slamming, cups started cracking, glasses started smashing and Audrey's world felt like it was spinning, never-ending, and her head rung with unknown voices as they filled her with an unpleasant feeling of fear and dread.

That was when she decided to try and put a stop to these strange happenings, although she didn't quite know what to do. Was this becoming the stalking of the living and the hunting of the dead? ...

Danielle Purvis (14)
Park View Community School, Chester-le-Street

The Anomaly

Something was wrong. He could feel it. Deciding to skip breakfast, he got dressed straight away. Afterwards, he walked out of the door towards work. Maybe he thought he would find some answers there. However, answers came to him as soon as he walked out of the door.

As soon as he stepped outside he saw it. The villagers were walking about, lethargically, unknowingly frustrated. Then he heard it: Disguised yet obvious. The faint humming coming from Wirend House, a dilapidated building on the outskirts of the village.

He was suddenly curious. He walked toward the building over the cobbled path. He shivered. What was this place ...? He opened the creaking door into a room. The few rays of light squirming in through the boarded up windows caught the dust floating about, giving an illuminated mist. He ascended the groaning stairs to another door, wooden, ornate. It was locked. The humming was louder here. What was on the other side? He peeked through the keyhole. A blast of white light knocked him backwards. The last thing he remembered.

You may wonder how I know all this. Well, he is me; in a way. At least, a part of me ...

Stephen Page (14)
Park View Community School, Chester-le-Street

The Hunt

Thud! Argh! ... Lois woke as she heard a scream from down the hall. The shivering squeal sent tingles down her spine. She reached under the bed for her Colt 45 pistol she had been given just the day before by her husband in case of any 'complications' they said. *Why has he given me a pistol?* she had thought. Obviously this situation was exactly what it was given for, whatever it was. She loaded the magazine and headed for the door. 'What is this place used for after hours?' she asked herself as she reached for the doorknob. *Click.* It was locked. Someone had locked her in from the outside. Whoever had done this, the fact still remained that she had to get out. She took two steps back and with a *thud ... bang!* she kicked the door straight off its hinges and headed down the hall, scanning the area with her torch-lit gun as she went.

Suddenly out of the darkness popped something gouged in blood groaning and stumbling as it walked. *Bang! Bang!* She fired off two rounds as it fell to the ground. She took a moment to analyse the situation and the thing that had just attacked her. It looked to be some sort of zombie-like creature with body parts missing. She heard a thud from across the hall and went to investigate but was greeted by the awful sight of approximately ten of these zombies feasting on innocent hotel goers. They had not seen her so she decided to stay out of sight, these things were literally ripping humans to pieces as if they were polystyrene. Regardless of the awful scene she was witnessing she had to keep quiet or else she would become dessert. But as some people say, the best means of defence is attack.

The hunt was on ...

Tom Parker (14)
Park View Community School, Chester-le-Street

The Moorside House

It was the late summer's day on June 11th 1944. War was on the brink of becoming hell! Russia was just a pile of debris, with the front lines on the verge of starvation.

One soldier, Boris Heqrevich, had been lost for 36 hours as he had parachuted off-target. No other contact. No food, no water. Despair was all he knew.

However, one house on the moorside appeared to leap out of nowhere. Alone and scared, he investigated, craving for just an apple or more so, a Hershey bar.

He entered. Cobwebs covering every corner of the room. It was abandoned. No one there. He hobbled through the house, while brushing his tipsy moustache with his brown, leather strap watch. A piano, he saw. Clean as a washed window. No dust on it, when everything else was covered.

His body beckoned into the next room, only to hear a noise. It was from behind! Mysteriously he knew the song. His brain clicked while realising it was his dead father's favourite tune on the piano.

'It can't be,' he whispered with lips moving from its parched drought. He ran back! But no joy came, nothing was there. An hour passed, then another and another, yet he hadn't moved at all.

Slam! Slam! again. The doors were closed and locked. Still no one was there. Then came a trick of the mind, or was it? As a voice leered out, 'Hello son …'

Chris Tyrrell (13)
Park View Community School, Chester-le-Street

Charlotte's Secrets

The wooden door slammed shut behind Emily as she crept into the attic. It was cold and too dark to see anything in the room. Step by step Emily quietly walked forward. She stumbled, head first, landing with a loud *bang!* Pain rushed through her body as she hit the floor. Carefully Emily sat up, holding her injured head, when she noticed something.

Damp, worn away and old. A small wooden box, with words engraved on the lid. Emily blew away the cobwebs and slowly read the words carved onto the box. What could this mean? 'Charlotte's Secrets' were the words on the dusty old box. Emily wondered what the words meant. Slowly she opened it and there lay a very crumpled-up note.

A cold shiver ran down Emily's spine as she unfolded the note. It was hard to read. Written in messy handwriting. Finally she realised it said: 'You have set me free, for that thank you'. Then the wooden box slammed shut, nearly trapping her hand inside.

That was it! She had to get out of the creepy old attic. Emily got up slowly. Turned her head. There it was! Pale and pasty-faced wearing a long white dress. A young girl stood before Emily. Jet-black hair covering her terrifying evil green eyes. She headed towards her. Petrifying face. Holding a knife. Emily screamed with terror. Trying to escape from the attic. Pleading for mercy. She turned her head. And it was gone.

Emma Robson (13)
Park View Community School, Chester-le-Street

I'll Miss You ...

Sunday

8pm   Watching TV and doing homework for tomorrow.
Laughing hysterically, Mother doesn't seem to get it though.
'What on Earth are you laughing at? You loon!'
'Can't you see it Mam?'
'See who? Oh, the TV, I didn't think it was supposed to be funny. Oh well, I mustn't be as cool as I used to be.'
Whatever! Like she was ever cool!

8.30pm *Bedroom* - Staring out my window. Lots of people out walking their dogs. Wish I had a dog, I would be healthier! I'll consult Mam.
'Mam, can we have a dog?'
'We'll see.'
She always says that! What does it mean? 'We'll see', it's so confusing.
I wonder how Grampy and Granny are? Haven't seen them in a while. 'Mam, when are Grampy and Granny arriving home from their hols? Have you heard from them?'
'Erm ... yes ... good ... night love!'
That was weird, it's 8.34pm! And when has she ever called me 'love'?

9pm   I'm *sooo* bored. And worried. Why was Mother acting so weird before? She really needs to get out more!
I miss Grandma and Grandad. I haven't seen them for a month. At least next time I see them they will have a present for me from their holiday.

9.15pm Bored, bored, bored!

9.35pm I've decided to confront Mam. 'Mam, why did you act so weird earlier when I asked about Gramps?'
'I didn't act weird honey!'
So it's 'honey' now is it! She's hiding something. Wow! Here comes Gramps now! Yey! That's a coincidence. I rush downstairs to see him. Mam stops me in my tracks.

'I lied before. Gramps is gone, he died this morning, I'm so sorry.'
Huh? But then what's that on the step? A letter, it reads: 'I'll miss you.
Love Gramps x.'

Madeleine Hutton (13)
Park View Community School, Chester-le-Street

Waking The Dead

Gabrielle moaned in her sleep. Every night she tossed and turned restlessly over a meaningless dream. Of course it was meaningless, she told herself as she managed to open her eyes and look at her clock. Oh no, 4am, she suddenly realised how pathetic she was being and went back to sleep.

Confused images spread like wildfire through her mind as her eyelids began to close. She was moving towards that glass ball, the glass ball that's filled with fire and with every step she took its power streamed through her blood, persuading her to step back and go. She couldn't not this time, she was going to find what it meant: she reached out to grab the blazing sphere. Danger.

At that moment she screamed in pain as she felt a fiery dagger go straight through her stomach. Her eyes opened as she realised the next chamber to her dream had just been released.

This is enough, she thought getting out of bed and walking towards the door. 'This is not going to bother me,' she spoke, with a sense of caution in her voice.

A stench suddenly filled the air and swarmed around her. Sensing that things weren't normal, she cautiously turned and within a metre was a figure staring at her in the corner of the room. She screamed but no noise came from her mouth. The figure floated over to her and simply said, 'You are needed now.'

Danielle O'Connor (13)
Park View Community School, Chester-le-Street

The Curse Of Heartstone Hospital

As I walked through the labyrinth of city streets, the giant building of Heartstone Hospital came into view. I must confess that the immensity of the place alone was intimidating, but I had a bet to win and a point to prove. The mammoth-like building dwarfed all others, and was the dominant feature on the horizon. It was unmissable, but it never quite seemed to stay in exactly the same place each night.

Upon arrival, I climbed the stone steps and noted the dilapidated exterior of the place. Crude boards had been nailed to the doors, so as to keep out any intruders seeking to loot the deserted building. Or, as some would attest, to keep out the creatures of Hell which lay within.

The heavens were sparse of stars, and blankets of menacing clouds traversed the skies. All was silent. Suddenly, the pearly white curtains at one window flapped erratically in the breeze and for a moment I swore that I saw a malformed, soul-divorced face.

No. The talk of revenants and ghosts was just children's rhymes and nonsense. Not to be defeated by planks of wood, I circled the exterior and, to my surprise, but not my delight, found an open storm cellar. Yes, you heard me; open.

The sounds of my steady feet and breathing were alone in the area save for a slight creak now and again. I spun around and gazed upon the outside world. Taking a breath of the dormant air, I turned once again to face the storm cellar door. My entrance was heralded by a shrill scream. This was not good ...

Ben Littledyke (14)
Park View Community School, Chester-le-Street

The North Street Massacre

Herbert awoke one morning in a pool of blood. He had bloodstained hands, bloodstained feet and bloodstained clothes. He looked around at this red puddle for about three seconds before he burst into hysterics. 'Argh!' Herbert cried.

As he looked around the room he could see that it was his bedroom. The blood wasn't just on the floor, but all around the walls, all around the ceiling and dripping slowly down the windows. *'Mum! Help! Mum!'* he yelled at the top of his lungs. Nobody came. Nobody answered.

He then realised that his sister didn't hear him. She hadn't yelled at him for screaming so early in the morning. He then realised that his budgie wasn't chirping, and his dog wasn't barking. He then realised that it would take a lot of bodies to accumulate such a large amount of blood.

Herbert ran out of his bloody room to an even bloodier corridor. He slipped, and fell down the blood-drenched stairway. He stood up and fumbled with the dripping, bloody doorknob. He finally burst out and ran around the street. Mr Finland wasn't watering his flowers. Mrs Joyce wasn't sunbathing. Nobody was anywhere or doing anything. He was utterly alone, soaked in the blood of the townsfolk of North Street.

Ben Nightingale (14)
Park View Community School, Chester-le-Street

Ignored

I wonder why my alarm didn't go off. Even Mum let me over-sleep. I feel really empty, not hungry, just like something is missing. 'Mum! You let me sleep in! Mum!' I holler down the stairs. Weird, she isn't answering, she must be down the shop.

Well, looks like I'm making my own breakfast. Walking downstairs, I feel almost as if I'm floating. I feel so light, this is strange. Cool, Dad must have fixed the creaky stair, it's usually really loud, but today it's silent. The whole house is quiet. Phew, noise, the television's been turned on: Mum must be in. I rush into the living room where I see Mum on the sofa. She's crying. 'Mum, what's wrong?' She's not even responding. She's practically looking straight through me. 'Mum! Stop ignoring me!' She's scaring me now. What's she doing? She's walking out and leaving me, I suddenly notice Mum's dressed all in black, that's strange, she usually dresses in bright colours.

Sobbing, I run after her. I don't like this, I don't understand what's happening. I scream Mum's name as I sprint after her, but I'm stopped dead in my tracks as I see Mum getting into a hearse. Spelt out in flowers is my name: Claire. What's happening?

Actually, that dream I had last night was quite scary. Me in the car, a bullet through my neck, screaming, sirens. Thoughts are firing around my head like lightning bolts in a storm. Oh no, one big thought crashes through the others. Am I sure it was a dream?

Zoe Neasham (14)
Park View Community School, Chester-le-Street

The Fat, The Smic And The Suicidal!

'I mean it, I'll jump!' yelled Mr Afro.

'Fine,' replied the police officer. 'I'm bored of this, now!' As he turned his back, Mr Afro was enjoying the last few moments of his life, hurtling down the side of a cliff. He was thinking about how good life was, when he decided he wanted to live.

'Someone fat get in my way!' he yelled to the terrified onlookers below. Mr Smic, who was really thin, and Fat Guy, who was really fat, were among them. 'Hey, fatso, get a move on!' came the shout from above. (Alright, so it was a really high cliff!) Offended by this, Fat Guy shoved Mr Smic into his path.

Now in most stories, Mr Smic and Mr Afro would both die, but this story, however, doesn't work like that!

What really happened was that a massive gust of wind blew Mr Afro, off-course, and he landed on Fat Guy. Mr Afro was fine in the end, even though the fire brigade had to be called to prevent him from sinking into the folds.

And so, to this day, Fat Guy lives with Mr Afro's footprints through each of his six stomachs and Mr Afro later jumped off a bridge, after hearing that his local McDonald's had stopped selling milkshakes. There's a moral in this … somewhere … let me know if you find it …

Andrew Shuttleworth (14)
Park View Community School, Chester-le-Street

Lights, Camera, Over

On the sixth day of the sixth month '06 William Howard sat down on his sofa in an apartment in central New York. After being at work he decided to put on a film from his vast collection. He put it in, slouched down on the sofa and started to watch. About half an hour later the film was reaching its climax and things started to happen. Strange things.

He was watching a horror film, which had not even been released yet, how he had obtained the film was a mystery. In the film there appeared the writing 'death is coming towards your door'. On the wall of what appeared to be a familiar apartment. At this time William was thinking, *unlucky for the person in that place, glad I'm not them.* He casually turned round to find the remote and then he was struck.

Struck by the blood-red writing on the wall 'death is coming towards your door'. This really got him worried. *How did that happen? What is going on?* were some of the many thoughts rushing through his head just like the blood racing round his body.

Unlike William Howard the film kept on rolling. The blood on the wall really disturbed him. *Bang!* A sudden crash on the apartment door made William jump violently. He definitely was in no state to answer it, so he just sat there as if he had just looked Medusa right in the eye. *Bang, bang.* Again the thing continued to crash on the door. Unnoticed by William exactly the same thing was happening on screen, just as if it had been through a cloning device. Silence. The banging had ceased. *Smash*.

Something had just burst through the door, what was it? The thing looked at William. William looked at it, but all he could see was a face full of emptiness and darkness just like before exactly the same thing had first appeared on screen.

The feeling of déjà vu was overpowering. And *cut ...*

Chris Watson (14)
Park View Community School, Chester-le-Street

The Magician's Locket

'Opening the door to your past is not the easiest thing to forget, you know there's no turning back once you're there.'

I took a deep breath; thought for a few moments and gave a modest nod of approval. Instantly I heard the locket click shut. The images in the room began to hurtle around me gradually starting to fuzz, constantly vanishing from my sight one by one. My body froze, lifting my feet from my old tattered shoes. Almost immediately I plummeted from the magician's office into what seemed like a never-ending tunnel of clouds, sky and fog. I soared through the dense air, gliding past rows upon rows of houses but quickly passed because of the immense speed I was travelling at. Finally, in the thick of the fog from afar I could see the extraordinary scenery that was ahead. The magician had explained what I should expect to see when I arrived although I was keeping an open mind on what lay ahead.

My body slowly began to recuperate its ability to move so I positioned my body upright and soon my feet were firmly on the ground. The tranquil sound of the flowing river nearby was peaceful as was the rush of wind that made the still trees shudder. It was beautiful. Though soon a deafening roar broke the silence. A clash of sound boomed from within the thick of the trees. Ever since I was little I had an eager streak to explore however today I was not so fervent. Slowly, I wandered into the trees reciting the terrible memories from that awful day, my awful past. Then, there he was, charging towards me. My blood pushed through me making my heart throb with pain. I fastened my eyelids tight. Was I crazy ... Probably?

Carley Jackson (14)
Park View Community School, Chester-le-Street

The Midnight Mystery!

It was a cold winter's night and I was freezing in bed, I couldn't keep warm. But if I got up to get an extra blanket, I could have woken everyone up. So I lay there, shivering, trying to ignore it. I had just drifted off into a light sleep, when suddenly a loud *crash* woke me up.

'Ella, for God's sake, shut up! You're always waking us up in the middle of the night! Get to sleep!' But it wasn't me, It can't have been. I was asleep ... wasn't I?

The next morning everyone was getting on as normal. Mum was washing the dishes, Dad was slurping tea and reading the newspaper, Michael and I were munching our toast and gulping down our orange.

All of us got the shock of our lives when, unexpectedly, a glass slid off the table and fell to the floor, smashing into a billion pieces. As usual, I got the blame. Everyone was yelling at me - no surprise there.

That very same night, everyone was asleep. Everything was peaceful; it was so quiet, you could have heard a pin drop. All of a sudden there was a horrendous noise. *Thud! Thud! Thud! Thud! Thud!* Now everyone was awake - and nothing was peaceful.

'Ella! go to sleep!'

Why do I always get the blame? It's not fair. It can't be me, it must be ... someone else. I was so tired, I closed my eyes, rolled over and went back to sleep.

'Ella! why did you sleep at the bottom of the stairs?'

Hannah Wilson (14)
Park View Community School, Chester-le-Street

Double Identity

Holly opened one eyelid lazily. She sat up suddenly after realising she wasn't in her small pink bedroom. Instead she was on a golden sand beach, *maybe somewhere in the Mediterranean*, she thought to herself. Then she remembered the horrific events from the day before.

She had been on her dad's boat. It had been fun at first. A laugh. A chance to finally spend time with him. After a while the sky went black and the waves got choppier. Panic struck the boat. The waves lashed at the sides of the boat. And then disaster struck! Holly felt the sharp tingling of the freezing cold salty water around her small body. The boat had been capsized causing Holly and her dad to fall in the unknown ocean.

That's all she could remember. And now she was on a deserted island alone. *Where's Dad?* she thought to herself. It was surprisingly windy for a Mediterranean island. She looked down where she was lying and noticed a brown crumpled piece of paper, slightly covered in sand. She picked it up.

'Welcome to Tempice Bay. Here is where your future lies. Follow the footsteps'. That was all it said. Holly looked up and sure enough small footsteps led up the beach and into a dank cave. What could this message mean? Who had sent the note and why did they expect her to be there forever? Holly got up slowly. She followed the footsteps until she reached a dark cave that had the strongest stench of dead flesh. She felt confused and afraid. She needed to find her dad. Holly crept into the cave. 'Hello!' she shouted.

'Hello,' it echoed back.

The further in the cave the stronger the smell became. The cave was so pitch-black she could not see what was causing the terrible smell. She fiddled in her pocket for a lighter. As she lit it and saw what it was she was staring at she almost fainted. She gasped, tears stinging her eyes. There staring back at her was her dad and herself lying dead on the cave floor.

Rachel Cook (14)
Park View Community School, Chester-le-Street

Murderous Mary

Did you ever hear about Murderous Mary? No. Well here's the story. Mary Jones lived at number 17 Lowfield Road. She was very ordinary. She went to church, looked after the kids and worked around the house with her husband. That was until her husband was brutally murdered. Yes murdered. And from that day she swore revenge on the little village of Great Lumley. At first it was just small things like kidnapping pets or stealing cars. But it got worse. She started to burn down houses and kill people. She fled many weeks later and when the police knew it was safe they moved in. They found her son and daughter strangled, stabbed repeatedly and shoved in a small freezer. The village paper boy had been suffocated and locked in a small chest.

Once the police had sorted it out Lumley went back to normal. Families went to church and paper boys delivered their papers. But they never did catch Mary Jones. Some say she fled to America, some say she committed suicide. But most of the town thinks she still lives in Lumley under a new name. And every suspicious death is her doing. So that's the story of Murderous Mary so … you better keep your doors and windows locked or you could be the unfortunate soul who is her next victim.

Ben Russell (14)
Park View Community School, Chester-le-Street

It's Going On

At school, something's about to happen, rumours are going around that school is being closed, but no one knows where it came from. The teachers are calling it the big deal but that's all. We would find out sooner or later.

Thinking about doing some investigating, going to poke around to see what's going on.

Thursday May 18th

School is getting very strange, pupils have just gone, teachers are passing messages in class to other teachers, pupils apparently haven't gone home and have never been seen since. Teachers are taking pupils out of lessons. They haven't come back for hours and when they do come back they're different, tired, they look rough but they don't make conversation. If you ask them something they just give a one word answer that you can't make a conversation out of, and if you ask about where they've been they just say they don't know what you mean.

Monday May 22nd

The teachers won't tell anybody anything, but look sheepish when they say it's the big deal and that we'd find out sooner rather than later. Followed someone who was taken out of class, said about needing the toilet, followed them, there were screams, then a whirring sound like a piece of machinery, the screaming stopped, then the camera in the corner of the room turned. Don't think it saw anything, went straight back to class.

Tuesday May 23rd

Getting close, think they're on to me.

Wednesday May 24th

May be the last entry, they're here …

John Luke Jane (14)
Park View Community School, Chester-le-Street

Glimpse

Steel and saliva mixed as the gun was pressed into the priest's mouth. A hand on his shoulder forced him to the floor. He gargled, attempting to cry out, but was silenced as the gun was pushed further down his throat.

A robed person towered above him cloaked and hooded in black, face shrouded in shadow, with nothing but two unblinking golden eyes staring malevolently down into his.

The Catholic priest closed his eyes. His teeth rattled against the metal, advertising his fear. Gathering up courage, he burbled. 'Wha-what are you?'

A glinting smile appeared beneath the hood, illuminated by the flickering candles of the altar. 'A reincarnation of a dead one,' hissed a voice. 'One who betrayed and murdered. One who took his life to hide from the guilt and dull the pain.' The voice trailed off, leaving a stunned silence. The reincarnation smiled. His master was right. The humans of today were gullible; they wouldn't recognise or remember him. His doubts evaporated; the plan would work.

Shutting his eyes, he embraced the pain as the gift worked its magic. Fresh wounds opened in his hands and feet, a spear wound glistened in his side. He reopened his eyes and looked down at the trembling priest.

'Child, this was a test!' He cast his gun aside and held out his arms in an offering of peace. The priest stared up at him with disbelieving eyes.

'Do you not recognise me?' Judas spread his arms outwards, blood now streaming from the holes in his hands. The priest gulped back a cry.

'Messiah!'

Simeon Mitchell (14)
Park View Community School, Chester-le-Street

Three Boys Ripped Apart!

Jay, Rey, Max and Jaws the husky were running away from home. They got lost so they were wandering around for somewhere to sleep. They came across a rundown barn.

'Shall we go in there?' Max suggested. 'It's better than a bush!'

'Look at Jaws, he's shivering,' cried Rey, bending down and stroking him. 'We have to go in!'

They decided to go in because it started to thunder and lightning. They didn't know what was gazing, gawping and gaping at them; licking its grim, black, bloodstained lips with a red tongue. 'The day has come again …' he chuckled.

The four walked into the barn. 'Quite cosy,' said Max. 'With all this hay we could make a bed for everyone.'

Rey heard a rustling up above his head. He looked up, a black blur scatted away. 'Gulp,' he gulped.

Jaws could sense something was up. He was trembling from head to tail.

Jay said, 'I'm going to get some hay.'

'I'll come with you,' said Max.

They went off. Half an hour later they came back … or so the others thought but only one did.

'Max where's Jay?' Rey asked.

'I don't know, I lost him!' He looked worried.

'Let's go and look for him,' Rey said.

Max went up a ladder, an old, rickety, rusty ladder. Two minutes later there was a scream, it made the blood roar in Rey's ears. Jaws howled like a starving wolf, baying at the moon. He sprinted out of the barn as if he had an extra two legs. The screaming stopped.

Rey took his hands off his ears. 'Jay!' he shouted. 'Jay, where are you?'

Nothing replied.

He went up the ladder and searched. His foot stood on something, it cracked and rolled away. A skull! He jumped and another crack, skulls and bones everywhere! But what was coming next was worse. In the lightning flash from outside he saw through the gap in the wall, two boys' bodies, Jay's and Max's; chests ripped open!

His nose detected something, it smelt like sick and rotten egg mixed together. He turned on his heel to find … two green eyes staring at him. It whispered, 'Human meat's the best to eat … kill … kill.'

Rey screamed. And his chest was ripped open! With two claws it took the beating heart from in his body!

Bethany Hill (12)
St Aidan's County High School, Carlisle

Charlie The Chair Meets Bobby

I'm Charlie the chair and I belong to Granny Alice, I have been with her for years, and we are both quite old now. But one day when I was sitting in my usual place, in the corner of the living room, I felt suddenly in pain. I had grown weak and old, I needed to be repaired. At that moment Granny Alice stepped in the living room and behind her was a huge fat man; he looked like he was 18 stone! I think he was called Bobby. Anyway Bobby handed Granny Alice some shining gold coins. *What are they for?* I wondered. Then Bobby came over to me and picked me up! I was being sold and for three gold coins, surely I'm worth more than that! 'I'm not going,' I shouted but humans can't hear me, typical!

Bobby with his rough hands shoved me into a van. 'Ouch!' I yelled. The pain was getting worse. After an hour of driving the van stopped next to a semi-detached house, he pulled me out, opened the door of the house and placed me right in front of a small TV that was old and broken. The room was cold and damp. Then suddenly my worst fears became true! He was about to sit down on me with his big butt! I would surely break if he sat on me! The tension was rising and I started sweating as the gigantic butt came closer and closer. No need to tell you what happened next. I now live in a garbage dump, broken and shattered.

David Armstrong (12)
St Aidan's County High School, Carlisle

High Rise

I woke up with a fright. I slowly sat up and looked around the pitch-black room. It felt like I was in a volcano and the lava was the darkness closing in on me.

Voices spoke to me, 'Help,' loudly like bells in a church tower that wouldn't stop. My throat began to feel dry and I started to smell fumes.

My eyes became accustomed to the dark. I could taste bitter chemicals. I was sweltering. Flickering illuminous lights flashed and danced around the door, paint on my walls started to bubble. I began to smell my own fear as sirens outside rang. Then it came to me.

Fire!

Without hesitating I jumped out of bed, the floor was as hot as the sun so I slipped my slippers on. I ran to the window, I ripped the blinds off the wall, it was hot but I managed to heave it open. The floors below had fire waving around out the windows. I screamed for help but the people below were without a doubt unaware of my existence.

My blood flowed rapidly around my temple searching for ideas. Then I remembered the ledge outside my window. I slowly climbed out and walked along to the rusty, wet, old ladder. The first grip it shook violently in the wind. I carefully climbed all the way to the top of the building.

A helicopter circled below. I started waving my hands and screaming, 'Help! Help!' It slowly drifted up. The only problem was I had to jump. It was a likely possibility that I wouldn't make it …

I lie here now in an endless coma, listening to people crying day in, day out, speaking to me, praying for me. But I know and I think they know the doctors will give up on me and pull the life support off. *Beep, beep, beep, beep* …

Danielle Cannar (11)
St Aidan's County High School, Carlisle

The Window

Mia, Emma, Lucy and Carla were walking around looking for something to do, as normal. They were getting bored of standing around doing absolutely nothing. They were just walking around and suddenly out of nowhere came a dark, deserted house that looked as if nobody had been there for ages. The gates were all rusty and the garden had no flowers or anything growing just dead plants rotting away. Mia, Emma, Lucy and Carla looked really scared. They didn't dare go in because they were scared. They pretended that they hadn't seen it and carried on walking.

The next day they went to school and they were still thinking about the house, they suddenly decided to go to the house and have a look around. So after school they went there and had a look around, it was dim and dark inside the house but outside the house it was broad daylight. As they walked through the door there was a big entrance hall with lots of doorways into other rooms. They went into a room and it had an old-fashioned bed with flowery covers on.

Suddenly they heard a howling noise, they thought that it was a ghost and they ran out of the room and into the main hallway, something appeared out of nowhere, it came right up to their faces, they screamed! Mia ran to open the window as she remembered that it was very windy outside. As she opened the window the ghost flew like a T-shirt blowing off a washing line. Mia, Emma, Lucy and Carla ran out of the house and they were never seen there again.

Amy Graham (12)
St Aidan's County High School, Carlisle

Charlie Chair

Hello, I'm Charlie, Charlie the chair. I have a horrific but quite funny story to tell you.

One day I was standing there minding my own business when a class came in, a fattish ginger boy came and sat on me, he has before but today as soon as he sat on me I just collapsed. He must have put on weight over the weekend. The whole class started to laugh but Mr Gobble didn't find it funny. He sent the fat boy out (he was called Tony) for breaking school equipment.

Over the next week Mr Gobble and the caretaker were having a hard job trying to find a piece of metal long enough so they could fix me. As I was so old anyway they were just going to demolish me but Tony, the fat boy, had found a perfectly sized piece of metal.

It took at least five hours to fix me but it was the most painful five hours of my life as a chair. The cold feel of the caretaker's hands as he kept touching my three chair legs. Then he got a big gun like tool with a flame on the end. He put the flame in the gap where there was no leg and I jumped in pain.

He was eventually finished. I had four perfect chair legs.

The next day I was being sat on by a taller, slimmer boy, there was no chance of me breaking with my new strong leg. Tom had to pay a fine of 50p that was a smaller fine than he would have paid but he did find the leg that mended me!

Ryan Johnston (12)
St Aidan's County High School, Carlisle

Basement Fears

One gloomy, dark winter night Ellie and Grace stayed behind after school to attend a dance. As it had finished they walked down towards the basement and they heard a strange noise coming from the basement.

'What's that noise?' asked Ellie.

'I don't know but let's find out,' replied Grace.

'Are you crazy?' screeched Ellie.

'No, come on it will be fun,' replied Grace walking towards the door.

They both went through the basement door, Grace ahead, Ellie trailing behind. They travelled down the stairs, the door slammed shut and locked the children in. They were so scared, it all went dark, then there was a whiteboard with lots of sums, Grace and Ellie were not the cleverest and they didn't understand who would do this.

'There's a timer … 59, 58, 57, oh no we have to finish the sums or we die,' explained Ellie.

'How do you know?' replied Grace.

'It says there,' said Ellie, pointing to the wall.

There was no time to lose, they did the sums then they had 1 left, they looked at the timer 10, 9, 8, they both panicked. Grace grabbed the pen and wrote an answer. It was wrong, then out of the locked door a ghost appeared.

'Marcie is that you?' asked Grace, while her hand was shaking and also she was a bit confused.

'I'm going to pay you back for what you did to me.'

'Eh?' said Ellie.

'You bullied me and then I got run over and you didn't even care so let's see how you like it.'

Marcie magically got a car from nowhere.

Ellie and Grace's hearts skipped a beat and they were sweating like anything.

'Please don't …'

It was too late, they were dead.

The next day their bodies were found, but nobody cared.

Katie Murray (12)
St Aidan's County High School, Carlisle

Ghost Dad

I first saw it two nights ago, the 5th of October.

I was walking alone, the wind rustled the leaves in the trees and I watched several twirl in the ground, I thought I heard footsteps.

I turned round, nothing.

I kept walking, but quickened my pace. Then I heard it again the defiant clump of boots walking against the wind.

I looked round, a black shape was hanging in the swirling wind.

I started walking faster until I was running.

It came after me.

I could still hear the creature as the wind whooshed around it. Or was that me?

I got a second glimpse of it. This time I saw the face. It was pale and ghost-like. Long, thin scars ran down to its chin. I studied the creature, transfixed by wonder and terror.

I tried to move my legs, they didn't budge. Long, greasy arms protruded from its cloak each as scary as the face. Cockroaches and maggots crawled through its flesh, making their home in its body. In its right hand it held a golden egg timer that swayed in the wind. My dad had one like it, it was his lucky charm, before he was shot.

I tried to run again, but I couldn't.

I screamed as ghostly hands descended on me. Then I saw the medal. Dad's medal. And I realised ...

'Dad?'

Ken Wiggins (12)
St Aidan's County High School, Carlisle

Escaping The Hood

It was a usual day in the Hood; drive-by shootings until on Friday night my house got sprayed! I can't stay in the Hood anymore. Who knows what could happen? Maybe tomorrow I'll have my back punctured with a 9mm.

So on Saturday I met up with ma homie Paul. I told him about ma house gettin' sprayed. Guess what, his house got robbed last night! We both agreed we've gotta get outta here!

So on that same day we headed down to the court on 5th Ave. We saw MJ and Jazz shootin' hoops. We asked them if they wanted a game of ball. We decided a wager for the game ... $5000 per head (this game was big money!) There was no rules, this game was going to be street!

I headed back to Paul's crib after that to get ma head down because it would be too risky heading back home. But that night I couldn't sleep, the game tomorrow kept ticking in my mind (it was a matter of life and death!).

I woke up around 6am next morning. I was dribbling the basketball outside. Paul came out onto the balcony. 'Are you nuts?'

I replied, 'Sorry man, how about I meet you down at the court?'

He moaned, 'Sure!' and moped back to bed.

I was on my way to the court when I spotted the guys that had sprayed my crib! I hit the floor and rolled underneath a Caddy. They walked straight passed me. When I was underneath the car I nearly shouted! The oil off the exhaust was dripping onto my face! They walked around the corner, I rolled out from underneath the Caddy, wiped the oil off ma face and sprinted to the court.

Later on Paul joined me and we ran through some plays before the game; then all of a sudden everyone stopped and stared. MJ had brought his whole crew down to watch.

I saw one of his homies with an indent on his lower back ... shaped like a gun! This was literally going to be a matter of 'life and death'!

The game started and we got to check the ball. I made an immediate sprint towards the hoop. I stopped, faked the shot and then laid Paul up the alleyoop and ... score! First point was to us (what a way to start the game). The game continued as it had started, physically and mentally tough, for both teams. They played dirty. I got elbowed in the face a couple of times and by the end of the half I had 2 teeth missin' and Paul had broken his nose! The score at the end was 11 to us and ... 13 to them. We knew the only way we could win was to score 21 points.

As the game kicked off again it was very much like the first half of the game. They called a time-out so we had to stop. The score was a tie 19-19, we continued again and I got the ball. I faked a shot, took a 3 pointer … score! We had won the game!

We took our money and headed home, life was going to take off from there! We moved into the flat that me and Paul had wanted as kids! We were just chillin' out when we got a phone call, it was Doc Martin! He'd seen us out on the court the other day and picked us for the squad. Our job wasn't to hustle it was to play first team NBA basketball!

I went back to Paul's house to pick up the rest of his stuff when I saw the people that sprayed my crib … dead!

Me and Paul had 'escaped the Hood'!

Jamie Sanders-Fox (13)
St Aidan's County High School, Carlisle

The Attic Monster

It was a dark and stormy night. Ernie and Rashmid's parents had gone out and left them alone in their big, black, creepy mansion. At first everything was so quiet you could even hear yourself think but what they never knew was that was all going to change.

They started hearing loud thuds from the attic, at first they just thought it was rats scuttering around but the second noise wasn't rats it was something a lot bigger. They approached the attic with an anxious look on their faces. Rashmid reached for the door handle and twisted; the door flung open. They paused for a second too scared to walk in. They finally worked up enough courage to step in. It was dusty and the atmosphere was palpable. They saw a shadow in the corner of their eyes. They glanced round and came face to face with the bogeyman. They lunged back screaming for help, but they shortly realised that it was no good.

They tried to escape but he blocked the exit. The bogeyman grabbed Rashmid and dragged him to the dark part of the attic and lynched him. Ernie was all alone against him. The bogeyman tried to take a chunk out of Ernie's ribs but he dodged him; he picked up the closest thing he could find, which luckily was a tool box, and whacked him over the head.

Later their parents came home and were distraught to find their loving son, Rashmid, had been hung.

Oliver Watson (12)
St Aidan's County High School, Carlisle

House Of Hell!

Anna approached the corroded gates and they opened swiftly. She advanced anxiously to the doors, which were oozing mould. They slowly creaked open to reveal a musky smell. The floor was covered in bones, which crunched under Anna's feet. All Anna could think about was spending a night alone in this wretched place.

Suddenly the lights switched off causing Anna to jump, nearly breaking the floor beneath her. Unexpectedly a loud shrieking scream echoed across the room causing shivers down Anna's spine. Anna edged towards the door but before she had a chance to open it, a ghost appeared out of nowhere; the ghost was laughing in a high, shrill tone.

'You can't hide from me you naïve little girl!' the ghost shouted. 'We're going to kill you!' said the ghost so viciously spit was flying everywhere.

'Argh!' bellowed Anna. 'Please don't kill me, I will do anything!' begged Anna desperately.

'We won't sacrifice your worthless life on one condition, you run around outside screaming 'I'm a little chicken' covered in feathers,' laughed the ghost.

'OK, deal but where will I find the feathers?' asked Anna.

'Over there in the cupboard,' said the ghost.

Anna moved nervously towards the cupboard. She opened the door and found the huge pot of feathers; she covered herself from head to foot. She darted towards the filthy door and started shouting, 'I'm a little chicken,' flapping her arms up and down. She bolted back towards the grimy door.

Suddenly a loud echoing noise screamed, 'Surprise! You're on Candid Camera.'

Chloe Ostridge (13)
St Aidan's County High School, Carlisle

Buckbeak And Unity

'I hear there is a £1,000 reward for capturing the unicorn or the hippogriff,' said Fred to Ted.

'Wow, really? We best start looking for them then shouldn't we,' explained Ted to Fred.

They grabbed their pitchforks and nets then fled out to the forest (the enchanted forest). Minutes later they were in the heart of the forest. Ted whispered to Fred, 'I think I just saw the unicorn!'

'Where?' whispered Fred.

'Over there … look there it is again,' whispered Ted.

'Oh yeah,' whispered Fred.

Let's go after it … but slowly and carefully, and …'

Crack!

'Oops!' said Fred,

'Try not to step on twigs, you moron,' whispered Ted sternly.

'Don't call me a moron, you moron,' said Fred, annoyed.

'Now the-… wait … listen…' said Ted.

Clip-clop, clip-clop.

'There it is,' Ted whispered quickly.

'Aye let's go get it,' said Fred.

'No wait, stay still and it will come to us,' said Ted, 'oh and Fred, be quiet.'

Just then they heard a *screech.* They spun around sharply to see … the hippogriff flying towards them at a speed faster than the wind!

'Hit the deck!' screamed Ted.

'What?' said Fred.

'It means; get down!' shouted Ted.

The net flew into the air and landed on Buckbeak! Buckbeak squawked and tried to fly but he couldn't, they had him captured. They both screamed, 'Yes, we have caught one!'

Unity used her magic horn to lift the net away from Buckbeak and onto the farmers, Ted and Fred! Buckbeak was freed and Unity flew away and Buckbeak followed. They became even more best friends than before and they were never seen again!

Catherine Louise Bolton (12)
St Aidan's County High School, Carlisle

The Broken Silence!

A scream broke the silence as two people dropped dead and the rusty gates slammed shut. The two young people ran to the church doors; as they got there the wind lunged the doors open, they ran in and soon locked the doors behind them as the wolf howled and the moon shone. They heard knocking on the door. They left. They looked out of the window as a hand appeared on the window ledge. They waited. A man pulled himself up, his torn face bled from the wounds; his mouldy flesh peeled from his face. They screamed! They felt cold breathing on the back of their necks. They turned to find an old man as the lightning struck and lit up the place as the blood dripped from his mouth to the floor.

The wind blew through the open doors as the chandelier swung left to right. The man stepped closer and closer to the two youngsters. They stepped to the side. They peered through the wooden doors to find a pile of mud at the open doors. They heard a shatter, they turned to find writing on the wall. It read … *You will die!*

They looked to the floor; they were standing in each other's blood! The blood poured out of the old man's punctured eyes as he grabbed their shoulders and started ripping the flesh off the youngsters. The wolf howled and they screamed.

Michael Ballantyne (13)
St Aidan's County High School, Carlisle

A Day In the Life Of A Piece Of Paper

Tip tap went the rain as I was sat on the desk. It was quiet as Miss Banks tidied the room.

'What a relaxing day,' I said to Pen. I'd kept well away from Shredder that afternoon.

'He's a bully,' complained Pen.

Soon after Miss Banks finished the cupboard, she came over to her desk where I was sitting. 'Hmm,' she said, 'this could do with a bit of tidying up.'

My heart sank, I didn't want to get moved. I liked this desk, I had a lot of friends there.

Slowly she put pieces of paper on a pile and dusted the desk. Then she put her hand close to me and she got closer and closer to the end of my desk! *Crunch!* She'd picked me up and bent one of my corners, I was in such pain! *'Help, Pen, help!'* I shouted to Pen. *'I'm in the pile and I think it's for the shredder!'*

'Wait there, don't worry!' Pen ran and used the ruler like a diving board. She landed on the pile of paper and set to work. One sentence, then two and soon it was a whole page.

'Done!' said Pen, who was very tired after all the work she had done!

Miss Banks came over ready to put the pieces of paper in the shredder but then she noticed that there was a beautiful piece of work on the top. 'I wonder who this work belongs to?' she said and put it in her drawer. Phew, what a day!

Bethany Windsor (12)
St Aidan's County High School, Carlisle

Mr Ghost

There was a blood-curdling scream. It was night with mist in the air but the full moon was lighting their way.

'What was that?' asked Jonny.

Both Mike and Jonny looked at each other; they looked around the corner. There was a shady figure floating around almost like a ghost.

'Is that a ghost?' whispered Mike.

'Of course not, there are no such things as ghosts, it is just a figment of your imagination!' proclaimed Jonny.

Then as quick as a flash it had turned and was flying at the speed of light towards them.

'Quick run!' shouted Mike, trying not to trip over gravestones.

The next day at school they were given a dare to spend a night at the old scary house by their school friends.

Later that evening the headed up towards the old scary house with their supplies, then in the house they put down their sleeping bags and amazingly went to sleep. At about half-past eleven they were awoken by an *ooh* sound. The ghost was floating around them.

'W-h-hat d-d-do y-y-you w-w-want?' stuttered Mike.

'I'm just a ghost; I have been trapped in this graveyard forever,' he said.

'Well why and why did you chase us last night?' asked Jonny.

'Well because years ago a ghastly flying committee did not want me in their group so they banished me to this place so that I would not be able to be in any more groups ever again. I'm harmless but on a night with a full moon I go crazy and kill and destroy everything in my sight,' Mr Ghost said.

Jonny went over to the window as he realised it was a full moon. Mike realised it was midnight; they both looked at each other and screamed, '*Aaarrrggghhh!'*

Jonny Brunskill (13)
St Aidan's County High School, Carlisle

Murder!

Billy-Joe decided he would go on a walk before he went to bed. John Lewis was also out there with his dogs, then all of a sudden he saw Billy-Joe fall to the floor! Then he saw someone run, he tried running after them, but he couldn't leave Billy-Joe alone in case he died. He ran back to Billy, he saw he had a knife stuck in him. He tried pulling it out and then the police stepped round the corner ...

The police saw him holding the knife in his body.

'Excuse me,' said one of the policemen, 'I am arresting you on suspicion of murder. You do not have to say anything but it may harm your defence, if you do not mention when questioned, something which you may later rely on in court. Anything you do say may be given as evidence.'

'Errrr, but Sir,' said John Lewis.

'I told you not to say anything, you can only speak when the tape is recording.'

'OK the tape is on, Sir,'

'Well I was out walking my dogs and I saw Billy-Joe, then all of a sudden Billy-Joe fell to the floor! He had a knife stuck in him and I tried pulling it out but then you caught me,' replied John Lewis.

'OK, do you know who could have killed him?' said the policeman.

'Urmmm, there is someone called Jayne Marie.'

'OK, thank you.'

'Excuse me, are you Jayne Marie?' said the policeman.

'Why, yes I am.' She hid her hand behind her back.

'Why is there blood on the floor?' asked the policeman.

'Urmmm, I don't know.'

'Come with me you are going to *Alcatraz!*'

Leanne Codona (12)
St Aidan's County High School, Carlisle

A Day In The Life Of A Lifeguard

Jack and his mam drove off down the hill to their lodge. They started to unpack the car and unpack their suitcases. The rain was pelting down. Jack was sitting by the window watching the rain trickle down the double glazed glass. They couldn't really do many activities in the rain.

'Mam, I'm bored, can we go swimming?' asked Jack.

'Yes OK then, go and get your trunks and a towel.'

They got changed and walked onto poolside. 'Wooh it's huge! I'm going to explore the deep end! See ya later!'

'Don't get yourself into any trouble!'

'I won't!' said Jack. He swam into the deep end.

The swimming pool had a tropical theme.

Meanwhile, I watched over him, sitting in my chair.

'Owww, help, I've got my foot caught, help!' shouted Jack. No one heard him. Suddenly there was a *clunk!* The wave machine switched on.

'Help!' screamed Jack, panicking. The bar started snapping, then another, then another. Suddenly Jack founding himself hanging off the edge of the drop down the tunnel. He was slipping. Then I saw what was happening to him so I dived into the water like a dolphin. He was just about to fall so I grabbed his hand but his hand was slippery and he slipped …

He was going further and further down the tunnel; his head was about a metre away from going into the machine; I had to do something, anything; I threw my whistle at the *stop* button. By this time everyone was panicking and staring. It was a direct hit; the machine switched off! Phew!

Rachael Denholm (12)
St Aidan's County High School, Carlisle

Horror On The Hills

In the remote country near Grasmere lived a family called the Wrights. They had no neighbours for miles. One night, when they were settling down after a hard day decorating, they heard a wolf howl. It sounded really close, so the father got up and shut all the windows and locked the doors. Then he saw it, it went straight past, a large dark figure walking past with four large wolves. Then he disappeared and …

He popped up in front of the window and tried to get in. Mr Wright froze as he looked directly into the wide bulging eyes of the man; the old man had grey hair, a large battered nose and only four rotten teeth. Then, as the wolves howled, the old man walked towards the back of the house. The man had only holey clothes on with a large pitchfork in his hand.

Mr Wright turned around to his family in disbelief; then it came to him; the back door was wide open for the dog was in the garden. Mr Wright ran across the house towards the back door, but it was too late, the old battered man was there right in front of them. The wolves ran in and raided the kitchen then went for the family. The man led Mr Wright back to his family and looked up. His bulging eyes were looking straight at them. The man took one step forwards, the wolves grew angrier and then …

Michael Smith (12)
St Aidan's County High School, Carlisle

The Holes

It had been a fantastic day. I had moved house and everything was ship shape but there were some holes in the walls.

It was the next morning; I climbed out of bed and changed. I was about to go downstairs when I heard a scraping noise. I turned around; it felt like someone was watching me. My heart pounded. I seized a pair of scissors that were lying on my dressing table. 'Who's there?' I whispered. Something caught my eye, a flicker or something, in the hole or through the wall. I reached out for the door, but just before I did the door swung open and hit me bang in the face. I flew backwards, unconscious and fell to the floor.

Later I woke up, there was blood dripping down my face and there was a pool of blood lying next to me. I looked around. then horror struck me; there was writing on the wall. In blood, my blood, it said: *You have five minutes to live!* Next to the writing was an arrow pointing to behind the wardrobe. I moved the wardrobe and behind it was a secret door. I opened it, and trembling, stepped in. The door slammed shut behind me. I was locked in. Something crept up behind and pushed me over. My scissors were still in my hand and I stabbed it and it fell to the floor, dead. I figured out it had been spying on me through the holes in the walls. I was horrified!

Carla McWilliams (12)
St Aidan's County High School, Carlisle

Bone-Chiller

A day in Monkey Universe's home.

It was in the dead of night, when David noticed an evil figure hovering outside. David went back to bed thinking that it was all in his mind, then the dreaded figure edged closer to the window, each time getting bigger!

It was now 3am and it was still pitch-black outside. It remained perpetual darkness, but the howling of the wind kept David awake.

Suddenly the door blew open and with a dramatic crash, the figure reappeared. David leapt up out of bed and thundered down the stairs and out into the storm. Gasping for breath, David ran into the forest, not thinking of what he would find. The evil figure pursued David into the forest, but lost sight of him due to the storm (and his vision).

After hours of evading the figure, David hadn't a clue where he was but did know that the monster was out there, somewhere. After a few hours alone in the forest, David thought that it was time to get used to forest life (or at least until he was found) but when?

Days and days went by but still no hope for David, but at least the monster hadn't found him … yet. David made himself a camp and lived on a diet consisting of mangoes, lemons, grapefruit, coconuts and frogs. How could he survive on a diet like this?

After a whole year in the forest, David lost 6 stones 1lb. Some say David was never found, but at least the monster was never found.

Christopher Gow (12)
St Aidan's County High School, Carlisle

J

It was 11pm. I was alone in the dark. I stepped outside into the icy cold. The wind caught my skin as if it was trying to rip into me.

I walked down the street and into the park nearby. As I stepped onto the hard cobbles, I saw a flash of light coming towards me. All of a sudden a car screamed when it braked about an inch away from my stomach. Then the car reversed and whilst doing so, it hit a bump. It rushed off into the distance, a trail of blood following it. I looked down at the ground and saw a mangled body, twisted and gruesome. I quickly bent down and touched his chest and when I lifted my hand, I saw it was covered in blood.

Then the distant sound of sirens caught my ear. I got to my feet and the police stepped out of the car. They grabbed my hands and cuffed them. I realised they thought I was guilty because my hands were covered in blood.

Now here I am, sitting in a lonely cell wondering how I got here, what happened? I am sitting on a rusty chair staring around me. There is a bed with smelly duvet covers and then there are the bars. Those dreaded bars that are stopping me being free. Those bars that make me feel sick. The feeling when I stare at them that I won't be going anywhere for a long time.

Those bars …

Abi Hetherington (13)
St Aidan's County High School, Carlisle

A Day In The Life Of A Football

'Hello Grass,' moaned the football.

'Hello Football,' replied the grass.

The grass and the football carried on talking, then the children came to play football.

'Here they come,' said the football.

'Oh no,' the net whispered.

The children kicked the football so hard the net was broken.

'Ah, ah, ah!' the football shouted, while the children kicked him.

'Please stop,' the grass moaned.

'Come in now,' the teacher shouted.

'Good job they've gone,' said all of them. It was a long day for everyone.

A new day had just begun for everyone. The children had just come to school.

'Rise and shine,' the football said.

'Morning,' the grass answered.

It was lunchtime at Granville School and the children went out to play football.

'More holes for me,' the net whispered.

'Don't worry,' the ball said.

The children did all sorts to the net. They had a good kick-about.

'Come in everyone,' said the teacher.

'Good,' the net groaned.

'I've got a surprise,' said the teacher.

'I've got a new net for you,' said the teacher.

'Yes!' shouted the net.

The net was replaced and everyone lived happily ever after.

Thomas Lawther (12)
St Aidan's County High School, Carlisle

Complete Fear ...

It was a cold dark night and the rain smashed against the window like a thousand demons trying to break and enter. Samantha sat alone in the room. The only other person was the man on the 10 o'clock news. It was pretty quiet until a large bang came from upstairs. Thinking about her small sister, Hannah, she rushed upstairs to check on her. When she reached the top, she glanced into the half-lit room to see her sister fast asleep. Suddenly, there was a flicker of the lights, then darkness fell around her. Fear rushed through her veins as it closed in on her. Then there was a creak, followed by another, then another and each one sounded louder than the last. She wanted to run, but she felt paralysed, her heart was pounding inside her chest. Then, *thud!*

She woke up and she could feel the hard wooden floorboards beneath her. She knew where she was but she didn't know how she'd got there. She slid back her hands and pulled herself to her feet. Something wasn't right and she had to find out what it was. She knew exactly how to do it. She slowly crept to the door and up the spiral staircase leading to the attic ...

Once her eyes adjusted to the dark, she started to rummage around until she came across a box. After sweeping off the dust, Samantha looked inside and pulled out an old newspaper cutting. As she read it, the hairs on the back of her neck stood up, and from then, she knew that she and her sister were not alone. She darted down the stairs like a bullet through the heart of a hunter's first kill and straight into her sister's room. Then a hand rested on her shoulder ...

Slowly, she turned her head and to her relief, her mum's face smiled in front of her. She was pretty safe ... for now!

Laura Bell (12)
St Aiden's County High School, Carlisle

The Three Knights

The journey begins

So, legend says that when a full moon reveals itself on the forbidden realm of warlord King Cragor, darkness will descend on the world. 1,000 years ago when knights rode on horseback and damsels were rescued from fire-breathing dragons, this very same legend was unleashed.

We start our perilous journey in a small town called Henchberg. We find our heroes in an inn, hooded, tall and armed. The first of our heroes is Airees, a skilful bowman who could shoot with great accuracy. The second, a man worthy of the gods, Maximas, was fierce, brave and deadly. Finally a sorcerer who had the knowledge of 1,000 men.

These 3 noble warriors ventured into the realm fully armed on horseback. The realm was dingy, dark and smelt of rotting flesh.

'Sorcerer, use your wisdom. Guide us through this maze.'

The sorcerer sounded out words in elvish, 'Es cal nos vich,' his staff lit. By doing this he revealed an army of undead skeletons.

'Airees, sorcerer are you with me in this fight?'

'Yes!'

'Charge!' Maximas roared as he charged to battle.

The skeletons were fierce but our warriors fought to the end.

A laugh filled the air around them, an evil, devious laugh and a man appeared. The man was sat at a throne and boomed, 'You'll never escape my realm!' then vanished.

Our heroes looked back and the skeletons were assembling themselves back together …

Robert Jenkins (12)
The Norton School, Stockton-on-Tees

Normandy

It was early morning in Normandy, about 4.30am. The sound of guns scared us all, the fog blanketed everywhere but we knew what we were doing. The noise was getting louder, we got off the boat. A shiver went down my spine.

'Get down, get down!' called Sgt Conrad.

A German bomber flew over the top of us killing one of our men. I realised that could be me if I wasn't careful. The Germans started to attack and we had a plan. Our plan was to attack and kill as many Germans as we could.

We were all camouflaged in green and yellow, our guns too. If we made it to where we wanted to be in time we could overpower this part of the land.

Private Joe King got shot in the leg. The medics came straight over. He might lose his leg. I ran into the abandoned house. I searched it with two of my men and we found some Jews. They said, 'We are hiding from Germans.'

We heard them shouting, 'Help us please, please help!'

We helped them out, unharmed, as the guns went off again.

I went out into battle, levelled up a German's head. 1, 2, 3 his head came off and blood went everywhere. I didn't know how I felt, but I knew I was doing my country proud. I looked at my partner, 'Watch out!'

I'd been shot. Would I survive?

Daniel Demoily (12)
The Norton School, Stockton-on-Tees

Playing With The Unknown

We were bored.

'Fancy a game of dares down the old harbour?' Liam said.

We knew we shouldn't but who would know?

It was my turn my dare was to enter the old abandoned ghost ship. I eased the door open it creaked and echoed through the ship. The door banged loudly behind me, I was petrified.

Inside the boat cobwebs hung like glitter everywhere. The huge chandeliers were broken and everything was covered in a deep layer of dust. Old artillery hung on the cracked, peeling walls. I stepped forward nervously, each step echoed loudly sounding like thunder. A loud shriek rang around the ship then silence. The hairs stood up on the back of my neck. I listened carefully, something was being dragged across the floor above. Footsteps followed and I knew it was getting closer.

Suddenly the door creaked open and in the shadows was a creepy old pirate. He hobbled through and grunted, 'Kill!'

My breath quickened and my heart hammered in my chest. I turned and ran but where to? I found a smaller door and crashed through it, knowing the pirate would follow.

I was in a cavernous corridor, not knowing which way to run. A door at the bottom had a shaft of light coming through. I opened it because the pirate was closer than anticipated.

I was safe and could see my mates on the harbour wall. I looked behind and sighed with relief. 'That was close,' I whispered.

Jake Large (12)
The Norton School, Stockton-on-Tees

The Children's Return

It was a dark, cold night. All forms of life had a chill down their spines. Thunder and lightning lit the black sky. It was a full moon and all you could hear was the creak of an old rusty gate which belonged to a block of flats.

The flats used to be a children's orphanage. No one lived in the flats because they had been too scared to sleep, too nervous to eat because of the noises and sightings that were heard and seen.

The orphanage opened in 1895. Around that time, families were very poor. Some of them died with not enough food to live on. The children went into the orphanage and never came out. Children that were naughty went down into the cellar with nothing but one slice of bread and one cup of water every two days. Most of the children that went down into the cellar died. Children that were alive down in the cellar had to put up with the rotting smell of old, dead bodies and rotting bones.

The orphanage was converted into flats in 1993 and no one has lived there for eleven years. People say the dead children still remain as ghosts.

On this very night eleven years ago, ghosts rose from the grave. The dead became undead and at midnight tonight they will rise and I will be joining them because I am one of them.

Help me ... please.

Eleana Evans (12)
The Norton School, Stockton-on-Tees

Camp Nightmare

It was a dark, stormy night. The trees scratched against the nylon tent. Wolf Creek Forest didn't seem quite like the friendliest place for a storm. Joe peeped his head suspiciously out of the tent. He felt he was being watched. He pulled his head nervously back into the tent. 'There is something out there,' said Joe.

Joe and Jake grabbed a torch each and crawled out of the tent gripping hold of each other. 'Maybe it is just a squirrel, or maybe a bird,' Joe quietly said.

'That is no bird,' Jake replied.

They got further into the forest. They saw a flickering light straight in front of them, what was it? They got closer and it stopped.

'What was that?' Jake anxiously said.

'Maybe it was a man, or maybe something else lost in the woods,' Joe answered.

Suddenly, they heard a big *bang*. It sounded like fireworks.

Wolves howled, birds fled. They thought it could have been thunder but it wasn't. It sounded like a girl desperately screaming for help. Lights flickered again. The batteries of the torches ran out. A strange shadow appeared in the trees. Another light flickered, the strange shadow got closer and they ran into darkness. They heard voices surrounding them. They felt cold chills running through the air, then silence. They saw a strange figure coming towards them. What was it?

Arran Musa (11)
The Norton School, Stockton-on-Tees

Haunted Mansion

One dark and windy night, when the trees were rustling and the wind was howling, Gilbert kicked his ball over a fence. He went to get it, but it went into a haunted mansion. Rumour has it that once you go into the garden, you never come back.

Even though the rumour scared him, he had to go and get his ball because he got it for his twelfth birthday. 'Here goes nothing,' he whispered. He ran around the garden like lightning, but he couldn't find it so he went into the mansion as slowly as a tortoise.

There were cobwebs hanging from the ceiling and wallpaper was curling off the walls. 'This must be a very old house,' he said as he was walking on the creaky old floorboards. He spotted a picture of an old man; he appeared to be a Tudor. As he went into a different room, the eyes of the picture followed him. He saw his ball but it was near the picture that scared him. He ran like a cheetah to his ball but as he was walking away, he hurt his leg and the picture grew arms and grabbed him. It dragged him in the fireplace underneath the picture and shot him out of the chimney. He went so high he touched the clouds. When he fell back down, he fell into a hot air balloon and was never seen again, *ever!*

Ethan Allison (12)
The Norton School, Stockton-on-Tees

Treasure Island

It was a dark, stormy night. There was thunder and lightning across the seas. The waves were roaring. The sand was swirling and it was raining like mad. There was rustling, screaming and shouting. The moon shone brightly. The sky stood still.

'Oh my gosh, what happened here?' shouted Ned.

'It's like a tornado has hit it,' said Trevor.

The pirates were going to an island which was in the middle of the sea. No one had ever been to this island. They didn't have a clue what it was, so this was the chance to find out …

'Brrr,' shivered Alice, 'it's very cold here.'

'You're right,' replied Mandy.

It was now dark and the pirates had nearly reached the island. The sails were moving rapidly and the waves were splashing against the ship beneath the black sky.

The next morning, the pirates split themselves into two groups and went to look for sticks and food.

Whilst Mandy, Alice and Sally were searching for sticks, Alice tripped over something metal. She called the others over to see what it was. They all started digging with their spades until … Sally found a rusty box. It looked like it was 1,000 years old. When they opened it they were very surprised to see treasure.

'Let's go and show the boys,' cried Mandy.

'Here come the girls,' said Peter.

'Look what we've found,' boasted the girls.

'Wow!' said the boys, amazed.

'I know, let's call this island *Treasure Island!*' exclaimed Stuart.

'Yeah,' everyone agreed.

Sadia Rahman (12)
The Norton School, Stockton-on-Tees

The Deserted Mansion

It was a dark, stormy night. Lightning lashed trees like a whip. A twig snapped. Wolves howled. The moon revealed itself. From behind the dark, mysterious clouds it shone. It was raining ferociously. Bob, John and Sue were looking for a place to stay. They found what looked like a deserted mansion.

'Is it safe to go in?' asked John.

'Yeah, let's go,' they shouted.

They headed for the large, deserted building.

Bob strode forward and waved the others on. 'Come on, you'll get soaked in this weather,' said Bob, commandingly.

They ran forward into the deserted mansion. They reached the mansion. The door creaked as Bob opened it. 'Come on in,' said Bob.

They entered suspiciously. It was dark, they couldn't see. They found a switch but it didn't work. They found a candle and lit it.

'Do you think anyone lives here?' whispered John.

They all went in the kitchen looking for food. All they found was ham, which they shared. Later, they went upstairs to sleep. There were two rooms. Sue went into one room and John and Bob shared another room. They slept a bit hard because of the weather.

They got up at 10 o'clock in the morning and went outside to check the weather. It was wet. The sun was shining brightly. They went to look for their tent because they had left everything they had brought in there. When they got there, they saw that their tent had disappeared. There was nothing left, nothing at all …

Arya Sepehr (12)
The Norton School, Stockton-on-Tees

The Little London Squirrel

It was about 3pm and I'd been woken up by a lot of loud noises. I climbed out of my nest and went to see what all of the fuss was about.

As I got closer to all of the noise, I saw football players playing on the pitch. I looked up at the screen, it was still 0-0. I was in with the home supporters and they were all cheering their team on, so I decided to go one step further. I decided that I was going to run onto the pitch and cause some problems, so I scurried through all of the fans and onto the pitch. The crowd went silent, then all started clapping and cheering.

I was getting chased by some stewards. They had a box, but oh no, I wasn't going in there. I decided to run over to Arsenal's manager who was eating some nuts. I ran up to him and then went back to my nest high up in the stand where I could still see the game being played.

The next day I was wandering around and I saw a newspaper on the floor so I picked it up and looked at the back page. *Wow!* I was on the back page, along with Sir Alex Ferguson, José Mourinho and Steve McLaren I couldn't believe it, and the headline was, 'Will the squirrel appear again at Highbury?'

The answer is yeah. I am going to run on next week for some more fun!

Josh Turley (13)
The Norton School, Stockton-on-Tees

Lost In Time

Clash! Clang! The sounds of clashing armour and swords rang around the arena as the two gladiators fought for their lives. The crowd watched, hypnotised by the movements of the gladiators and the sun glinting in their eyes.

'Kill! Kill! Kill!' they chanted, as Ragus, the famous Roman gladiator, closed in on Defalys. He brought his sword upwards, ready to make the crushing blow, but suddenly the crowd fell silent. Ragus looked around. The amphitheatre had vanished. He turned to his opponent, who was still cowering on the ground.

'Get up, Defalys.' He didn't move. 'Get up! Can't you hear it? Something's happened and you're cowering on the ground!'

Defalys turned, and seeing Ragus wasn't joking, he got to his feet. 'Where are we?' he asked.

'I wish I knew to tell you,' Ragus replied. 'Now get moving!'

Together they moved towards a nearby forest, fascinated by the size of the trees. Suddenly, a wolf bounded toward them out of the forest. Instinctively they drew their swords, but the wolf stopped inches in front of them. Then it turned, half walked into the forest and stopped.

'What d'you reckon?' Defalys questioned.

Ragus didn't answer, but took a step closer to the wolf. As if in answer, it took a step into the forest.

'We follow it,' Ragus answered, and set off at a sprint after the wolf. Defalys followed, and together they sprinted into the dark forest after the wolf. Suddenly, without warning, the ground opened up and swallowed them ...

Jennifer Parkin (13)
The Norton School, Stockton-on-Tees

Horror At Camp Norton

One dark, spooky night at Camp Norton, there were fifty people around a campfire when suddenly a person noticed a misty figure in the tree behind their instructor. He was watching it come down as a howl bellowed through the trees, then the campfire went out. When the young person looked back up, the figure had disappeared. The instructor lit the fire again, when the young boy saw the misty figure again. It looked as if it was coming towards them. The instructor started telling ghost stories.

The young boy looked down then looked up, hoping that the figure had gone again, but it hadn't. The young boy tried to warn everyone, but they wouldn't listen to him. As the misty figure got closer, the boy could see its empty eye sockets, its broken nose and its three black teeth. The young boy was hoping that the misty figure would go before it got them. Then they heard another howl bellow through the trees and the campfire went out again. But the instructor didn't relight it, all he said was, 'Let's go to bed and get some rest because we have an early start in the morning.'

The young boy went to bed but he couldn't get to sleep because he was worrying too much about the misty figure. As he was nearly asleep, the door mysteriously creaked open and a misty figure stepped through the door. He attacked the young boy, but the other people didn't hear because they were asleep.

Paul Phillips (12)
The Norton School, Stockton-on-Tees

The Adventures Of Kratos

Kratos jumped off the ship and met the crew in the port where he greeted the crew and they spent an hour getting prepared, and finally set off to the middle of the Aegean Sea.

On the way they stopped off on a deserted island for food and water. Kratos and five other crew members set off for food, but as they set off, screaming came from the ship. They sprinted off towards the ship and there was the revolting serpent, *Hydra,* attacking the ship. So Kratos got out his swords and ran in for combat. He leapt ten feet in the air onto Hydra's back and started to slice its vertebrae, until it grabbed his foot in its yellow, serrated teeth and threw him at a great speed onto the deck of the ship.

Then the statue advised, 'Let it eat you, then you can slice out its bowels, thus killing the beast, and you'll escape.'

Kratos took the advice and leapt into its mouth and hung onto the side of the stomach. He started to carve its stomach like a carpenter with an oak tree and the beast just dropped down dead, with Kratos cutting his way out of its carcass. The crew sailed back to Athens. The trip was terrible, there was a storm which killed half of the crew, but when they got there, the crew just disappeared and Kratos went to Mount Olympus and became a champion warrior of the gods.

Daniel Matthews (12)
The Norton School, Stockton-on-Tees

MNI (Mission Not Impossible)

Mission: Retrieve the golden coin.
Agents: 0011 Jim, 099 Bob.

MI4 Headquarters

P:	'The golden coin is located at the bank in Germany.'
Jim:	'What is the name of this bank?'
P:	'It's called The Bank.'
Bob:	'OK, so we are going to the bank in Germany.'
P:	'Yes, Money Pound has your tickets inside.'
Jim:	'OK, we'll be back in a week with your golden coin.

They left the meeting to get a head start on the mission.

Jim:	'There is only one ticket here.'
M Pound:	'Well one of you will have to be snuck in in the suitcase.'
Jim:	'Well not me. Bob, you're going in the case.'

They left headquarters to get to the airport.
They walked to the taxi station.

Jim:	'Give me your mobile.'
Bob:	'I don't have it.'
Jim:	'Well give me 30p.'
Bob:	'I have no money.'
Jim:	'Go in that shop and get change.'

Jim sat down on a bench to wait for Bob, when he saw a golden object roll past him.

Jim:	*'The coin!'*

Jim chased the coin down a hill and it stopped in a crack.
Jim picked it up and walked back to the bench.

Bob:	'They had no change for a fiver.'
Jim:	'OK.'

They got in a taxi and paid with the coin.

Jim:	'That coin looked familiar.'
Jim and Bob:	*'The coin!'*

Taxi drives away …

Christopher Burdess (13)
The Norton School, Stockton-on-Tees

Worst Day Ever!

Dear Diary,

Oh, I have had the worst day ever; first I totally embarrassed myself in front of Dean Williams, the cutest boy ever. Then something terrible happened in science …

Let's start at the beginning.

It started out as a pretty normal day, you know, the usual get up early, can't really open your eyes much but anyway then I went down for my breakfast.

After breakfast I got ready and I was set to go. 9.15 and I was ready to go as usual.

On the way to school things were normal and I got to school just in time.

Tutor time was OK, except stupid Terry Jones just wouldn't shut up. Oh he gets right on my nerves. Anyway, let's get back on track. As I was walking out of tutor, that's when it happened …

I was walking down the corridor as normal and then it just came out! I couldn't help it! A strange noise came from behind me and everyone started to laugh, and then I realised that it was me who had made the strange sound! Oh my God, now I knew what I'd done … I ran as fast as I could, I didn't want to stop, I felt so embarrassed!

Now let's get on to science. Science was normal until Sir announced that we had a project and I soon feared the worst, *partners.* I always get partnered with the worst partner, but this time I wasn't!

Or so I thought …

Laura Wilkinson (13)
The Norton School, Stockton-on-Tees